Copyright © 2022 Christopher P Jones.

All rights reserved. No part of this book may be reproduced in any form or by any electronic or mechanical means, including information storage and retrieval systems, without permission in writing from the publisher, except by a reviewer who may quote brief passages for review.

This book is a work of fiction. Names, places, characters, and incidents are either the product of the author's imagination or are used fictitiously. Any resemblance to persons, living or dead, is entirely coincidental, except where the reference is to public domain information on that person.

Reference to countries, events or locales are used merely to add an element of realism to the story. The use of historical events is based on information in the public domain.

Second edition 2022
First published 2020

Thinksheet Publishing

www.chrisjoneswrites.co.uk

Vanished in Berlin

Books by Christopher P Jones

NOVELS

Berlin Tales Trilogy:
Berlin Vertigo
Vanished in Berlin
Berlin Vengeance

ART HISTORY

How to Read Paintings
Great Paintings Explained
What Great Artworks Say

Vanished in Berlin

Christopher P Jones writes historical, mystery and literary fiction. He is fascinated by the possibility of opening up a window onto the past. He is also an art critic and art historian.

Vanished in Berlin is his second novel. The first instalment of the Berlin Tales, *Berlin Vertigo*, was published in April 2020.

To find out more, go to www.chrisjoneswrites.co.uk

Vanished in Berlin

VANISHED IN BERLIN

By
Christopher P Jones

Vanished in Berlin

PROLOGUE

Vanished in Berlin

1

Berlin, Germany. 1931

Hermann Graf von Hessen pulled the chord on his Wagenfeld table lamp and watched the milk-coloured glass flicker into life. The light dispersed across the desk, illuminating a framed portrait of Adolf Hitler on one side and a bronze model racehorse on the other.

It was eleven o'clock at night and Heidelberger Strasse outside was empty. Hessen turned to his bookcase and reached for his accounts book, just as the sound of a car engine hummed outside and the beam of a pair of headlamps rose towards the ceiling.

He lifted the window blind to check outside, then firmly drew it shut. Grabbing two bullets that were stood upright on the desk, he loaded them into the chamber of his Luger pistol as he heard the opening bolts of the main door echo through the corridor on the floor below. He slid the pistol into a drawer as the click of footsteps approached up the stone staircase.

The thickset frame of Gustave Jan Ringel entered beneath a semi-circular archway. He had intense eyes, a broad forehead and an expression of reigned in confidence.

Hessen rose to his feet and looked at his guest with a

look of indignation.

Ringel glanced down to the gorget patches that newly adorned Hessen's uniform collar, showing two oak leaves against a black background.

'Oberführer,' Ringel said sternly, acknowledging Hessen's recent climb in status.

Hessen remained still and tight-lipped.

'So you now look after the whole of the Berlin SA?'

Hessen took a long pause. 'If I do, you'd better beware.' He then drew out the pistol from the desk drawer and pointed it at the other man.

Ringel looked at Hessen sharply, then lifted his forearms into the air in an effeminate manner as if to surrender, at which Hessen burst out in sheer laughter.

'My friend,' Hessen replied, putting forward his hand to shake. 'As if you didn't see it coming,' he said as they both sat down on either side of the desk.

'Bravo. You're getting good at this.'

'That's thanks to you. Now I'm looking forward to getting to grips with the scale of the appointment.'

'You must celebrate.'

'Well, I have a new Mercedes on order. Speaking of which, a modest loan may be required, if you will oblige?' Hessen discreetly closed his account book to cover over a credit note from Diskontobank.

'I will have my secretary ring you tomorrow,' Ringel replied without thinking twice.

'Of course. Now I have another matter I wanted to discuss with you.'

Ringel picked up the photo of Hitler from the desk. 'Are we safe to talk here?'

'Yes, we won't be disturbed.'

Ringel laid the photograph face down on the table. 'Then tell me, what is on your mind?'

'The Vendetta project. The proposition is shaping up

well. I just need your assurances.'

Ringel nodded before going to the far side of the room where a three-pronged candle holder stood on a mantelpiece. He struck a match and lit all the candles, then ceremoniously carried the object back to the desk. It was all performance, typical of Ringel.

'When I'm on stage,' he said, 'I impress people with being able to read their minds through hypnosis. I persuade them that I can communicate with the dead. But it's just a trick. The human brain is actually quite easy to fool, and it's not difficult to find participants who are susceptible to suggestion.' Ringel waved his hand through the three candle flames as if to test their temperature. 'The important thing is to create a convincing illusion.'

'I don't need tricks,' Hessen replied soberly. 'I have my own nerve.'

'Of course, but show me anyway.'

Hessen moved his hand above the flame of the middle candle and held it there. The flame licked the underside of his palm like a thirsty tongue. He looked up at Ringel, whose expression remained frozen solid. Hessen kept his hand over the flame until his arm began to tremble. The muscles in his jaw tightened, but his hand remained in place. Finally, with a suppressed gasp, he pulled his hand away and plunged it into a jug of water as he screeched wildly. He lifted his head and caught Ringel's eye.

The clairvoyant nodded slowly and said, 'There is nothing to be concerned about. I have consulted the star charts for your future. Vendetta will not fail.'

Vanished in Berlin

PART I – ARNO & MONIKA

Vanished in Berlin

2

'Mark my words,' Herr Goldstein said, looking out of the window. 'There is unrest out there. Those who move against our community are becoming more murderous and we must be vigilant.'

Monika Goldstein was sat curled up in an armchair whilst her father laid down the law. It was the same speech she'd heard a dozen times before.

As a criminal lawyer, Felix Goldstein considered himself well acquainted with the worst malefactors of Berlin. His most widely-reported case involved the successful conviction of two insubordinate youths. Their crime was the brutal slaying of a seventy-seven year old man, a killing that was not only unnecessarily bloodthirsty but all for the measly gain of thirty reichsmarks. The pair, who had clearly targeted the old gentlemen, now found themselves in Berlin's Plötzensee Prison where they awaited punishment, almost certainly the guillotine, so long as their state-appointed defence lawyer couldn't find a loophole.

'You have to trust me, my darling,' Herr Goldstein went on, standing on the hearth of the fireplace, trying to catch his daughter's eye. 'There are parts of this city you must steer clear of. Especially after dark.'

Monika squirmed in her seat but she didn't protest.

She had always been taught to act with caution but things seemed to have moved up a notch. Although she was attending college now and had entered young adulthood, she remained forbidden from courting any boys that her parents had not previously vetted. What was a mystery was if they were ever going to let her make her own choices.

Then the clocks of the house started to chime seven o'clock. 'Is that the time? We better be going. Are you ready?' Her father rubbed his hands together, prompting Monika and her mother to rise to their feet. It was Friday and the synagogue on Fasanenstrasse would be filling up quickly. Herr Goldstein preferred to arrive early as a mark of respect to the rabbi and was keen to depart right away.

'Actually, I'm not feeling well,' Monika said. She held her cheek with the back of her hand. 'I don't think I can go.'

Frau Goldstein rubbed her daughter's hand and felt her brow. 'You do feel a bit over-warm. Will you be okay on your own?'

Monika nodded whilst her parents looked at each other. 'You go, I don't want you to be late,' Monika said, as she saw herself climbing aboard one of the electric trams that wove through the city or else taking a U-Bahn that rattled beneath the streets. Her mind was calculating which would be the quickest.

'Fine,' her father said after a pause. He checked his watch. 'You rest, darling. We won't be late.'

A few moments later, Monika was closing the door behind her parents. She grabbed the felt-covered hot bottle she had been sitting on, then ran up the stairs to her bedroom and got changed.

Meanwhile, Arno Hiller was counting out a stack of

banknotes in his attic room where he lived, inside the pitched roof of an apartment block. The cash came to sixty marks in fives and ones, which he slipped into the fold of a silver money clip and then sauntered down the spiral staircase to the street outside.

The money came from the sale of a manual printing press, a heavy machine that had been hanging around his attic room for two years and had the proportions of a gramophone player. He desperately needed the cash, which is why he had been stubborn on the price, even when the buyer – a paunchy man with a face like a fist – had begun to grow jittery.

With sixty marks in his pocket, Arno emerged out onto Baruther Strasse. A quick turn to the right and the world of Café Kaiser opened up before him like a resplendent dream. By day, Café Kaiser was a bustling affair, drawing in the local townsfolk – the street-sellers, dressmakers, pawnbrokers and lawyers on their afternoon break, as well as the occasional tourist who'd wandered off the beaten track.

By night the bar came alive in a different way. Glowing red table-lamps and the sound of a saxophone playing provided a ruby-like prism for the menagerie of drinkers, soldiers, actresses, gentlemen and con-artists who gathered there. Weaving between them came the local prostitutes, eyed-up by shadowy men who lounged and slithered like reptiles, waiting for the right hour to make their strike.

Arno didn't flinch at the atmosphere. He was young and impulsive. It suited a man like him to come to a place like this and mingle with the nighttime rabble from the many walks of life. It was especially instructive after the midnight hour, when there would be dancing, cross-dressing and feisty camaraderie between strangers. It would all happen when twelve o'clock came, like a reversed mirror image of the day.

There was only one type of company he didn't enjoy at Café Kaiser and that was when the Brownshirts came in. Every evening, five or six SA Stormtroopers would turn up carrying collection tins, which they thrust under the noses of every table. At this point, the prostitutes slipped into the shadows and their customers buried their faces into their drinks. For the next few minutes, the only sound was the silvery splash of coins being dropped into the metal boxes. Everyone was obliged to give, and if anyone happened to be short, they would have to rely on a friend to lend them a few marks, with the words 'I'll pay you back when I can.'

Tonight the Nazis seemed particularly charged up. Apparently, there had been a big meeting at a local sports ground and now the men and boys – all of them dressed in brown and black uniforms – were streaming back into town. They were hungry, thirsty and twitching with zeal.

'Mind out,' Arno said instinctively as he blithely strode through the frosted-glass doors of the bar, practically knocking over one of the Brownshirts. The collection tin he was holding slipped out of his hand and scattered what seemed like a thousand coins across the floor.

Rising quickly, the eyes of the Nazi were grey and fixed as he squared up to Arno. He stood with his hands tightening into fists and a pot-belly spilling over his waistband.

'I don't have any money for you, so don't bother asking me,' Arno said. He wasn't afraid, mostly because he made a point of being intrepid and could withstand a punch if it came his way.

'Not so fast,' the Brownshirt grumbled as he signalled for support from his companions.

Arno turned to find five other men coming towards him. He glanced between their faces to see if he recognised any of them. He might have done. He'd believed in their cause once and had performed the raised arm salute enough times, but not anymore. He was aware of their propensity for terror and disorder, and no longer cared for their brand of violent earnestness.

By now most of the bar had noticed the confrontation and were looking over. 'You have no business here,' Arno retorted. 'The police ought to lock your lot in prison.'

The Brownshirt gave a bitter laugh before lunging at Arno with two open claws. Arno dipped to one side and escaped the full force of the onslaught, wriggling free of the Brownshirt's attempt to snag his jacket. He knew his way around the bar and had just about outwitted the gathering troop of Nazi gang members when another one blocked his path. Arno charged forward and managed to thrust the Nazi into an open cellar door just metres away in the floor behind him. As he zigzagged through the room, hurling himself over tables and benches, he launched towards the exit ahead of him. He clattered through the glass doors and out into the street, just as he heard one of the Brownshirts call out, 'Next time, you're dead.'

Arno made a dash for the nearby U-Bahn. Before he got there, he caught sight of Monika coming out of the very same station. He'd planned to meet her at Café Kaiser but now it was no longer possible. It was no place for a Jewish girl to come, certainly not tonight.

He composed himself, took her arm and walked her in the opposite direction. 'It's such a beautiful evening,' he said, straightening out his shirt, choosing not to mention anything of the incident in the bar.

'Where are we going?'

'There's been a change of plan. I want to take you to the Kurfürstendamm.'

It was summer. The country was in full bloom and a walk along the lamp-lit avenue of the Kurfürstendamm was perfectly inviting. The atmosphere was vibrant, the way the café terraces brimmed with people and the sound of music trickled from every doorway. As they looked into the shop windows, they found each other's hand and let their fingers entwine, if only for a minute. It felt forbidden to let their hands meet and link among the evening crowds. For once they let their guard down.

A moment later, she unthreaded her hand from his and whispered, 'What if someone sees us?'

'Why should it matter?'

'It shouldn't but things are difficult for me. We must be discreet,' she said, lowering her head.

'Look at me.' He swept a lock of hair from her brow. 'I just want to be with you. Out in the open, not needing to watch our backs all the time.'

'I want that too, but we can't.'

'Come with me. Let's slip away together.'

Monika then seemed to blush a little, but the look in her eyes said it all.

3

A week later, Arno woke to the feeling of warm sunlight spread upon the contours of his back. Monika lay asleep next to him in the hotel bed, her hair unbound and wrapped around the arc of her shoulder. The day before they had taken a train out of Berlin and found themselves in this tiny little town. It was a wild kind of liberation, to be nestled in the hidden folds of a rural hotel where nobody recognised them, where they could be unseen and unhindered.

He was proud of their courage. Here they were able to share their love in public without restraint. He was no longer Herr Hiller and she no longer Fräulein Goldstein. This weekend they were pretending to be *Herr und Frau*, 'just-married' and drinking in the pleasures of their union under the guise of a honeymoon.

They had left Berlin from Anhalter Bahnhof. The last thing they'd seen as they stepped onto their train carriage was a troop of teenage boys marching in files of three through the station, with short trousers and socks pulled up to their knees, boys who had mastered the solid clap of feet against concrete, copied from their Nazi heroes. The boys smacked their boots against the floor as if they were in competition with each other, filling the steel and iron hall with chilling reverberations. That was the way they did things in those boys' clubs.

Just about every activity, no matter how big or small was turned into a tournament between the members.

Arno knew what went on in those youth groups. He'd been on the camping trips and taken part in the war games in the woods. And he'd sat up late into the night, having torch-lit conversations about the excitement of war and the disappointment of having missed out on the last one.

Politics had lost its shine since then. The way he saw it, everyone hated everyone: the Communists, the capitalists, the Jews, the gentry, the army, the landlords, the farmers, the unemployed. It was a binge of loathing, and nobody had any way of bringing it to an end. He was glad to leave it behind. Berlin, the city of sunshine and hatred, was all but forgotten.

In the hotel room, he rolled onto his back and thought about how his views had changed. His past wasn't perfect and he had told Monika only so much about it. He glanced over at her. A Jewish girl? It didn't matter to him one bit. Not anymore. She was warm and soft laid next to him. She was beautiful and quick-witted. That's what he saw in her.

The early morning light through the window dimmed as it shifted and a cloud went by. He nudged her by sliding his leg back against the weight of her foot. He would remember the weekend for these moves under the bedclothes.

They lay there in the yellow-amber glow of the sunlight, gently waking, half-smiling, still dreaming. He moved towards her, putting his hand on her knee, and slowly pressed his palm up along her thigh. Monika began to smile, her eyelids still shut as she murmured, 'I'm still asleep.'

'Is that so? I have other plans for you,' he said, nuzzling himself into her.

'I'm getting up now.' She loosened his grip with a sly tickle in his ribs. She blinked rapidly as the sun caught her face. 'Besides, I have a surprise for you later,' she said, shading her eyes whilst rising from the bed before he could catch hold of her again.

Arno grinned and watched as she disappeared behind the bathroom door. He sat up, lit a cigarette and then rolled out of bed. He checked himself in a mirror before putting on a shirt and a pair of trousers. As he braced himself up, he put his hands into his pockets and noticed that his wallet was missing.

It was a square leather pouch with a fold-over flap. He always kept it in his trouser pocket, but it wasn't there. He searched through his coat and then through the satchel that contained their things for the weekend, but it didn't turn up. Next, he crouched down on the floor and searched beneath the bed. The wallet had all their money; without it, they would have nothing to buy food with or pay the hotel bill at the end of their stay.

He stood up and in his mind, he began to retrace their movements from the day before. The train station, the small restaurant where they ate schnitzel, the square with the fountain…

There was nothing else he could do: he would have to go out and look for it straight away before someone chanced upon it and claimed it for themselves. He slipped out of the hotel room with Monika still in the bathroom, cushioning the heavy weight of the door as it swung shut to stop it from banging.

The hotel lobby was a gloomy hall with wooden stalls and medieval-looking furniture. There was a huge iron candelabra hanging from the ceiling that looked as if it could kill ten people if it fell. Arno hunted around the place, when he heard a voice call out to him. He looked up to see a slim woman dressed in a chambermaid's uniform approaching him. 'Herr Hiller this note arrived for you just five minutes ago.'

Arno was puzzled. 'For me?'

'Yes sir,' she said passing it over, as she rolled a laundry trolley away.

Arno opened the folded paper and read:

'Herr Hiller,

I believe I have found your wallet. Please come to the war memorial straight away so I can return it to you safely.

Yours,
Herr Poelzig'

Arno felt relieved and thought twice about going back to the room to tell Monika before heading out into the town. If he was quick then she need know nothing about it.

It was a tumbledown place, with narrow passageways and crooked houses made of timber beams. Searching for the rendezvous point, he could soon see the top of the memorial up ahead. As he walked up a cobbled slope he came upon a man in a black fedora hat sitting on an iron bench facing the monument. When the stranger saw Arno approaching, he quickly rose and tipped his hat emphatically, before he disappeared into a winding alley. With no chance to ask if he was Herr Poelzig, Arno frowned and then realised there was a wallet on the seat where the man had been sat. Undoubtedly it was Arno's but when he opened it to check on the money inside, it was empty. Damn! The cash had been taken, every last pfennig. *Gottverdammt*!

He went after the man along the snaking alley and stopped only to find there was no trace of him. Arno kicked the brick wall and marched back up the path. Now he'd have to go back to Monika and tell her that things had changed. She wouldn't like it but maybe she wouldn't take it as badly as he thought. Knowing Monika she'd be straight onto a plan B. Only, they'd have to run from the hotel without paying and get themselves onto a train back to Berlin, preferably unnoticed. To him, that sounded rash but necessary.

In this spirit, he returned to the hotel feeling just as resolute as when he left it fifteen minutes ago. Yet when he got back he found the room door had been left open.

'Monika,' he called out.

But there was no answer. Inside, both the bedroom and the bathroom were empty. Monika had vanished.

4

Arno searched the hotel room. None of her clothes or personal belongings appeared to be missing and the room looked just as it did before he went out. There was the small brown satchel-case left on a chair and their few possessions strewn about the room. Monika's hairbrush was still on the dressing table. Nothing seemed amiss. He went into the bathroom. Nothing strange here. The only thing he noticed was that the bristles on her toothbrush were still wet.

What would have caused her to go out? Maybe she had gone to speak to the hotel staff about something and forgot to shut the door? Or maybe she'd gone to look for him? There was no note from her to explain her whereabouts – it didn't seem to be like her to go off without a word. Not like he had just done! He thought twice about leaving the room in case she came back, but after twenty minutes there was still no sign of her.

Eventually, he went out and scouted the corridors of the hotel. He went to the foyer and into the little paved courtyard where they'd taken a drink the night before. Monika was nowhere to be found.

Next, he took to the streets of the town. Every hour, the clock in the main square chimed and a little wooden man holding a trumpet wheeled out mechanically. There were plenty of passageways, shadowy corners and medieval nooks that could easily make a person invisible. He tried to imagine where she might choose to go. He expected her to jump out at any moment, and that gave the search an edge of uneasy excitement.

The town was smaller than he thought and he quickly covered the entire length without finding her. Before he knew it, he passed beneath a stone wall and found himself looking out over open fields. He turned around and went back into the town, beginning to feel that something was wrong, especially as he felt sure she had no money with her.

It was so hot that morning and the sun above seemed to tremble with brightness. As the hours passed, he began to become more alert to the town around him. Of the few restaurants, cafés and shops that dotted the place, most were closed. Some girls in pinafore dresses with grubby aprons were kicking a stone around in the main square, chasing after it and laughing. A man in a cap reprimanded them and they ran away. An old church loomed overhead, its three spires rising like a devil's fork in the sky. It was quaint but there was something eerie about the place too.

Arno went back to the great stone wall at the end of town and looked out across the empty stretch of farmland that led to a forest in the distance that was dark and huge. He began to feel Monika was getting far away from him and decided to go back to the hotel hoping she may have returned there.

When he reached it, the thick wooden door was sealed shut. Ringing the bell that hung by a metal rod came to nothing. A notice on the door said it was closed until seven that evening. He hunted through his clothes for a few seconds, gouging through his empty pockets for the room key he knew he'd forgotten to pick up. He hoped that another guest might arrive and allow him to slip in with them, but nobody came. Nothing stirred inside the building, no simper of life, just the reverberations of his fists against the big wooden door.

He took hold of the back of his neck feeling frustrated, when suddenly the door opened and a small somewhat disgruntled lady answered. He explained he'd forgotten his key, rushed past her and made his way back to the bedroom. There was still no clue as to where Monika was. What had happened to her? Had she had second thoughts about the trip? He knew she was nervous about what her parents would think of her absence…

As he considered these things, he sat on the chair next to the dressing table and noticed something catching the light from the window. Leaning forward he saw the glossy surface of a photograph pinned beneath the bristles of her hairbrush. Arno was sure it wasn't there before. When he picked it up, he leapt up realising it was no ordinary picture. What it showed was a row of four Nazi SA men, easily recognisable by their uniforms and cloth caps. And to his horror, there was Arno himself, who stood on the far left with the other three men stacked up next to him. The photograph must have been taken some four years before when Arno was in his late teens, a chance snapshot at one of the rallies he sometimes went to. He had no recollection of having the photo taken; but there he was, vivid in black-and-white print.

What he didn't know was how it got into the hotel room? Had Monika seen it? It seemed irrefutable that she had. Was this the reason she was gone now? He went to check the satchel-case where their train tickets were kept, and just as he suspected, the tickets were gone. He had no choice but to believe that Monika, in her haste, had taken both tickets and returned to Berlin on her own.

He couldn't stand being inside the hotel any longer, so he gathered up the rest of their belongings and pushed them into the satchel. Then he left the hotel without paying for the room. Twenty-five minutes later, he was standing on the station platform waiting for the Berlin train.

The station was empty except for a pair of women smoking on a bench and a small stray dog curled up in the opposite corner. The board showed no arrivals and just a single departure: to Berlin in two hours time. He asked one of the women for a cigarette. She gave him two. As he lit up, he blew a plume of smoke into the sky above which was turning a shade of peach.

He couldn't wait to board the train and return to Berlin. He had no ticket, but then again, most of the time on these rural trains there was no guard to check. He would take the risk. That was the sort of person he was. He didn't mind taking a risk.

Unfortunately, the train was a slow-mover and would take all night to reach Berlin. But what choice did he have? Besides, it would be easier to travel unnoticed at night. He decided the journey would be a chance to take some time to think. He simply had to get back to Berlin and tell Monika the full truth about his past. There was no point in keeping it from her any longer. By tomorrow, he'd be back in Berlin, back with his sweetheart.

5

Arno crept silently along the train corridor, looking for somewhere to keep a low profile. The train was eight carriages long, with sleeper cabins in the first two. He found an empty compartment in the fifth carriage along, pulled on the sliding door and slipped inside. The train started up. He felt sure he hadn't been seen as he nestled behind a wall of wood panels and glass. Lifting his feet onto the opposite seat he put his head back and shut his eyes, thinking if he could get to sleep the journey would be quicker.

But he was wide awake. An hour passed and the summer evening turned dark. Outside, bright electric night-lights shone and died, spinning orange webs under his eyelids. He looked out to see where the lights were coming from. Sometimes they illuminated an open tract of land, sometimes they brought the world up close, a brick wall or the sudden mouth of a tunnel.

After a few stops, he could see more passengers getting on and plenty of people on the move. His mind then pushed on to Monika and how that old photograph no longer represented him. He had to set the record straight with her. There was no chance he would join the Nazis again. He was done with them.

Just then, he watched with disappointment as the door to his compartment rattled open and a couple edged in. They brought with them numerous bags, which they took a great deal of time to squeeze through the door and hoist onto the luggage nets overhead. Arno found them hard to ignore, as he lifted his legs off the opposite bench.

The man sat down with a thump. He was mean-looking, with a crooked nose and a bald head. His eyes were inset with dark hollows like the depressions of teacup saucers. He wore a suit that was loose-fitting on him or else so old it was warped at the elbows and knees.

Meanwhile, the woman preened herself in the oval mirror that hung above the seats. She wore a cream raincoat with a cream belt tied around the waist. She kept the coat on as she sat down and crossed her legs. Arno could see she had fresh skin and wide, arching lips.

The strange couple settled into their seats and spoke in quick sentences. The man was complaining to the woman for bringing too much luggage. She changed the topic and blamed him for choosing second-class when she would have preferred first. He told her there was no first-class on this train. She told him flatly that he was wrong and expected better.

Arno attempted to shut out the squabbling couple by standing up and pulling down the carriage window to let in some of the nighttime air. The couple then fell silent as the train started moving. Sitting back down, Arno glanced at the pair, who now seemed to be at ease with one another.

After ten minutes, the man got up and declared he was restless and was going to walk the length of the train. He balanced with the swaying of the carriage, tottering in his baggy suit through the sliding doors and out into the corridor.

Now, with just the two of them in the carriage, the woman suddenly sat forward and held out her arm. 'Feel my pulse,' she said, out of the blue.

There could be trouble here, Arno thought. He reached forward and put his thumb against her wrist.

'Is it fast?' she asked.

He felt nothing at all, not even a beat. 'You seem fine to me.'

'I had too many shots of coffee earlier.'

He moved his thumb to pick up the merest trace of life. Eventually, he found a pulse; it was quick and bold.

'Tell me, is it racing?'

'It is a bit.'

'You think so? My head is spinning.' She plunged into her purse, searching for something she didn't find.

'Would you like me to shut the window?' Arno asked.

She gave a faint smile, as though her thoughts were suddenly pulled elsewhere. Then curiously she asked, 'How would you like to make some money?'

The question caught him sideways.

'Well?' Her eyes glared as if the answer should be perfectly obvious.

'How?'

'Do me a favour? For me and my boyfriend? If you do us a favour, we'll pay you.'

A series of half-formed thoughts came to him, twilight thoughts, graveyard thoughts.

'What do you want me to do?'

She leaned forward and whispered, even though there was no one else in the compartment. 'Listen, if anyone comes through here asking, pretend we haven't spoken and we don't know each other. That's all. Just act like we've never met before.'

'Well, that's easy,' Arno said, remaining poker-faced. 'We never *have* met before.'

'Exactly!' The woman grinned.

Sooner or later the stink-faced boyfriend returned, all puffed up and wobbling. He was eating some pungent food from a fist of newspaper. As he sat down, he briefly gave a knowing look to his girlfriend, who nodded back. Without further consultation, he put his hand into his pocket and took out a small sheaf of notes which he slid across the tiny table fixed beneath the window.

It was all planned out, Arno thought. Still, since he was broke and the money was in front of him, he put his palm over it and lifted it off the table. The man lit a menthol cigarette, and asked, 'You live in Berlin?'

'Yes.'

The man then handed the package of food to his girlfriend, who buried her head in the paper and took an enthusiastic mouthful. It was like she hadn't eaten in days.

'You've lived there for long?'

'For a little while now,' Arno said, trying to reveal as little as possible.

'Good. And you're travelling alone?'

Arno's thoughts turned to Monika. It wasn't supposed to be like this. He wasn't supposed to return to Berlin alone. Still, wherever she was, he wouldn't want her in any part of this.

'Yes,' Arno confirmed.

The ugly dog fixed his eyes on him. 'Do you have a train ticket?'

Arno scratched his ear lobe. 'Yes, don't we all?'

'Let me see it.'

'Why?'

'So we know we can trust you.'

'You'll have to take my word for it.'

'In that case, you better hand the money back.'

Arno casually flicked through the bank notes showing he wasn't prepared to part with them, at which the man started to grimace.

'Enough,' the woman said. 'Give it to him.'

'Here.' The man took out a leatherette wallet and from it a slip of paper which he threw on the table.

'Now you have one.'

Arno saw it was a ticket to Berlin. 'Thank you,' he said, feeling smug.

'Now hand it back.'

'What?'

'The ticket. Give it back to me.'

Arno passed the ticket back to the man, who stood up, unzipped a side pocket on one of his bags and slipped the ticket inside. It was the last in a row of six bags they had in their possession, the one directly above Arno's head.

'You'll stay with us in this compartment. With your ticket. Got it?'

Arno tilted his head in agreement, remaining aware of the money in his pocket.

'And this bag' – the man used his cigarette to point to the bag with the ticket inside – 'is yours, right?'

'Whatever you say.'

'It belongs to you whilst we're travelling together. Understand?'

Arno glanced behind him and upwards. The bag was a brown holdall with gold fasteners snaking around its corners. It had bulges along its side, solid lumps as if a stack of bricks had been forced inside. What could the contents be? Books? Cigarettes? Maybe something dangerous even? 'I'll guard it with my life,' he said with a hint of sarcasm.

The man smiled and revealed his teeth, which were remarkably white and perfectly aligned. When he smiled, some of his ugliness lifted and he took on a more elegant bearing.

'It's full of children's toys,' he said, turning to his girlfriend and smirking at her. She smiled back.

Bastards, Arno thought. Whatever was in that bag, it had to be bad news.

'One last thing: if you get into trouble,' the man said, 'say the word *Vendetta* and we'll step in.'

Arno looked at the man, not trusting him an inch.

'Say it,' the man insisted.

'Vendetta,' Arno confirmed coolly, knowing he'd taken the bait.

Presently, the train was pulling into a station that was lit up like a cinema screen. There was dried seafood and salami strung up in shop windows. People on the platform stood with bags and suitcases ready to board. Arno began to expect a guard to come aboard, and the thought of it made him feel slightly tense. The train moved on, taking its passengers deeper into the night.

Finally, a refreshments trolley came through. Using his new money, Arno bought a sandwich and a large brown bottle of beer. There was no guard, no uniformed bureaucrat, no petty official. The beer went down quickly. He thought about getting up and finding the same drinks trolley and buying a second bottle. But leaving the compartment seemed forbidden.

An hour passed. The man opposite started to snore, purring loudly like an enormous cat. He pushed out his legs – two imperialistic feet that intruded on Arno's corner.

Arno tried his best to remain awake and alert to the couple's movements, but he drifted off before waking again at some unknown hour. Everything was murky. His mouth and eyes were dry. He looked out of the window and could see a dark blue mist climbing. It was the very first minutes of the morning.

He looked at the couple opposite. They were both

asleep. The man's mouth was slung open like a sagging hammock. The woman was more in-between, her head lolling on her neck as if her eyes could snap open at any moment and catch him watching. He thought about getting off at the next stop and slowly stood up to reach for the bag above him. He'd entered a deal and had their cash in his pocket, but now he wanted the ticket and had no real intention of earning either.

But it was too late. Before Arno could find the bag he glanced behind him to find the woman staring at him. She shook her head as if to suggest it wasn't a good idea, like she was frightened. So Arno thought he'd refrain, for now at least.

Instead, he pushed his head into the corridor. He noticed some of the overnight passengers had been replaced by morning commuters into the city. They had combed hair and smelled of tooth-powder and perfume. The morning sun was low and white, flashing into the carriage like a lunatic lighthouse. The atmosphere had changed now into something more familiar: the brisker logic of daytime.

Then, at the far end of the next corridor, through the adjoining doors, he could see two guards working their way towards him. He returned to his seat. It was time to gather himself and play the part assigned to him.

The man opposite was beginning to wake. The woman, who was now caught in the natural light and seemed fractionally less glamorous than the night before, set her glazed eyes on the passing countryside through the window. The gorilla next to her bore all the marks of a shabby night's sleep: puffy eyes and slack cheeks, twitching with some sort of agitation.

A minute later, one of the guards stepped into the compartment. Arno looked up expressionless. The guard looked back and forth. 'Are you three together?' he asked, waving his finger between Arno and the couple opposite. The guard had blond hair and a gold tooth winking from between his lips. In his waistband was a pistol and a small black baton.

'No,' Arno replied. 'We don't know each other.'

'Okay.' The guard put out his palm to the couple, 'Tickets please.'

The man slipped his hand inside his jacket. He brought out a slip of yellow paper, which to Arno's eyes didn't look like a ticket. The officer took some time to examine it, then as if prompted by something he'd read and consequently understood, looked up to the row of baggage in the nets above their heads.

'Do these belong to you?' he asked the couple, pointing.

'Yes.'

With the flat of his hand, he felt along the broadside of each bag. He was more perfunctory than really searching for something, as if he was just going through the motions. Then he turned to the bag above Arno's head. He reached the brown holdall and began fondling the misshapen leather, pressing and clasping at every swelling.

The woman said quickly, looking at Arno, 'That's his.'

'Yours?' the guard asked.

Arno feigned a smile.

'Ticket please.'

Arno got to his feet and lifted the bag down onto the bench seat. He was both tired and hot with adrenaline but he didn't show it. He couldn't be sure where the man put the ticket, so with his back turned to the guard he went to unzip one of the side pockets. The fastener stuck at first, so he had to wrench it back and forth until it opened. For a split-second, he expected to find something rotten inside, like a stack of Soviet bank notes or a live snake. Instead – as he glimpsed quickly – he saw there were dozens, maybe hundreds, of little purple and blue books. Passports. They were bundled into stacks of around twenty in a batch, bound up with rubber bands.

He drew the side of the bag together quickly, sure they were for the black market. His crumpled up ticket was not there, so he opened the flap at the other end, where his ticket flipped out like a jack-in-the-box. He handed it to the officer, who appeared to initial it on the rear side and then passed it back.

'Now. Show me what's in the bag.'

'There's nothing of interest in there.'

'Open it please.'

Arno returned his fingers to the main pocket of the holdall. He loitered, glancing around, realising there was nowhere to escape to, so he loosened the mouth of the bag. The guard stepped closer and opened it wider, peering into the gaping hole. The passports were in plain sight now.

At this, Arno looked to the couple opposite who appeared to be oblivious to what was going on.

'What are these?' the guard demanded.

Arno said nothing as he stepped aside.

The guard had his hand inside the bag now. 'What are these?' he asked again, more gravely this time.

Arno stood motionless for a moment, before he declared the keyword, 'Vendetta.'

The guard looked at him blankly. Arno's eyes darted to the ugly brute and his girlfriend. They were ignoring him altogether. Their eyes were on the guard. They must have heard him say it. His eyes flickered over to the guard.

'Care to say that again?' the guard replied.

'Vendetta,' Arno said with a deliberately blunt

cadence.

At this, the guard's expression changed. His face seemed to turn pale by a shade and his mouth began to sag a little. His gold tooth hung in the morning air. He closed up the bag and gently, almost caressingly, fastened up the pocket. Then he lifted the bag back into the netting where it came from and stepped back by a pace. The guard bowed his head, gave the thinnest of smiles and then silently left the compartment.

Arno was stunned. A coolness passed through him, a tight, swirling blend of relief and satisfaction. He sat back on the bench and looked quizzically at his fellow travellers.

At once, the couple opposite got to their feet. 'You did perfectly,' the man said. His voice was more brisk than before, as if he'd just woken up and was his real self again.

'Well done,' confirmed the woman. Was she being condescending?

'What just happened here?' Arno asked.

'We got what we wanted,' she replied. 'We suspected this train line was a route for smugglers into the city. Now we've just proved it.'

The couple were lifting their bags from the racks, preparing to leave the train. Outside the compartment glass, along the train corridor, another man appeared, someone they knew, who now began to assist them with their luggage.

'Who are you?' Arno asked forcibly.

'We're with the Prussian Police,' the woman replied.

Arno immediately felt uncomfortable at the idea.

'It took guts what you did,' she said.

Arno stared out of the window, perplexed by what had just taken place.

After what seemed like just a few minutes, the train

began to slow. The next moment, the windows were filled with the smoke and blather of Berlin's Anhalter station. All through the carriage, people were gathering up their belongings and shuffling towards the carriage steps, elbowing each other, impatient to get off.

In the spin, Arno switched from his compartment and onto the train platform. A surreal feeling took hold as he made his way through the morning crowds. He half-expected to see a confrontation or arrest by more officials – police? guards? soldiers? – or whoever that couple on the train were connected to.

Were they the Prussian Police? If they were they must have been working undercover and Arno had unwittingly aided their investigation. And the corrupt guard on the train? He'd be for it now and whoever else was involved.

Still, Arno thought, the whole charade was over now. He was free and had money in his pocket humming to be spent. That's how it often went for him: one day his luck would be down, the next day up. He wasn't a stranger to acting in clandestine ways or being in some sort of fix. And he'd never once come to any real harm. Not yet anyway.

He couldn't wait to see Monika now, to restore her faith where she had been given cause to doubt him. He went into the great city, sure she had returned, sure he would find her safe and sound.

6

Arno stepped out into the plaza where the train station opened up to the city. The sky was smoky blue and the sun was steadily climbing, and all at once he felt reinvigorated. The morning air was laden with the sweet smell of roasted almonds on charcoal braziers, and there were people everywhere, men in their trilby hats and women in their close-fitting dresses sweeping along the pavements.

After nine hours on the train, he had a compulsion to move and get to his apartment as soon as possible. But first, he found a local bar that served breakfast. He ordered a plate of fried eggs with bratwurst and jam relish, along with a large cup of *Milchkaffee*. He polished the meal off in haste and reconvened his way home.

The tram to Hallesches Tor was crowded. Pushing his way on, he balanced against the motion of the carriage and concentrated his mind on Monika. He recalled the last time they were together in his attic room, when she'd turned up clutching a bag of food from the market to her chest, ready for lunch and a happy day ahead.

'What shall I tell my parents?' she'd asked when he suggested the idea of a weekend away. The initial excitement had quickly stiffened into concerns and questions. She twisted her fingers through her hair, pondering the spontaneity of it all.

'Just lie,' Arno said in response.

'How? They'll want to know where I'm going. I can't tell them I'm staying in a hotel with you!'

'Tell them it's a camping trip.'

'I never go camping.'

'Tell them you've joined a youth group. I was part of one once. They go camping and hiking all the time.'

'They won't believe me. My parents are suspicious of those groups.'

'Tell them you've made friends with some steady Jewish girls.'

'No, that won't work. They'll want to know their names and where their families live. You don't know my parents as I do.'

'Can you think of something else?'

As he sat down, she propped her folded arms on top of his shoulders and gazed out of the window, thinking how liberating it would be for them to be somewhere they wouldn't be recognised. 'Of course,' she said, standing up with what seemed to be an obvious idea. 'I could say I'm going away with my drama group.'

'Your drama group?'

'I joined quite recently. There are plenty of things you don't know about me, Arno Hiller.'

The memory of that conversation looped through his mind as his tram rumbled across the city. He thought about Monika's parents. They *had* believed her story in the end. The tale about a trip with her drama class had worked. Now, if they knew she was missing, they would be fraught with worry.

Arriving at Hallesches, he passed over the square where the trams criss-crossed each other and motorcars circled round in great bending loops. It was only a five-minute walk to his attic room from here. Realising he had nearly a hundred marks on him, he decided to conceal his pay-off and stow the cash away.

He made his way up to his room, up the staircases with their split wooden floorboards and wobbly banisters, towards the top floor and the hatch in the ceiling. It was cheap but he liked it there, his space in the clouds, like a belfry in a church tower.

But when he reached the hatch he found that the padlock was broken. Within seconds, he pushed the flap upwards and over, and moved furtively up the final few steps to the top. Inside, he saw the table had been pushed aside against the old stove, leaving a mess of smashed crockery below it. Around the corner, he found the bed had been overturned and the mattress split open with a knife. There were pillow feathers scattered across the floorboards everywhere. And the walnut cupboard had been prised opened, making it clear that its contents had been rummaged through. The only things left undisturbed were his bicycle and about three-dozen bottles of beer, most of them already drunk.

He looked through the window, down onto a patchwork of rooftops and an army of chimney stacks. 'Why turn this place over?' he thought to himself. He could only think that some opportunist had slipped into the building and tried their luck while he was away. It wasn't the first time the apartment block had been targeted by thieves.

He checked around and found nothing of any value was missing. Not that he had much of value anyway. Then, placing the cash in a tin box under the floorboards, he repositioned the capsized bed over the top of it.

The last twenty-four hours had been strange. When he thought about the business on the train with the police and the passports, part of him wasn't surprised.

He was no stranger to Berlin's underworld; the city was teeming with smugglers if you knew the right people. But he'd never been used by the police like that before. And what did the codeword *vendetta* secretly mean?

He washed his face, changed his clothes and lay down on his mattress. From his pocket, he took out the photograph he'd found in the hotel room. He loathed the way he appeared in it, with his self-satisfied grin and Nazi colleagues pressed up against him like they were blood brothers. The idea that Monika had seen the photo and glimpsed into this aspect of his past disturbed him.

Knowing her as he did, he knew she wouldn't have taken the decision to leave the hotel lightly. She was strong-willed but underneath it all, she was a deeply level-headed person. Her parents had instilled that in her.

Then he thought: maybe she had gone straight home and was presently safe in the reassuring company of her mother? He suddenly imagined her describing the photograph and how she now felt betrayed. Meanwhile, her father would be stood nearby, offering a consoling voice, 'You'll never have to see that wretched boy again.' Arno's name would be dirt.

What would she think of him now? The other burning question was, who had put the photograph in the hotel room in the first place and why? His mind fizzed with unanswered questions. And for that reason, he had to go there.

7

When Arno arrived in Schöneberg district where Monika's family lived, he pressed on with zeal. The next few minutes would shape everything: either Monika was at home and their relationship was seemingly done with, or she was elsewhere and his search for her was only just beginning.

Before knocking on the door, he thought about her refusing to see him and the possibility of him forcing his way through to her. It didn't matter to him that Monika's father was a lawyer and her mother had all the air and graces of a lawyer's wife. He had to talk to her.

Their street was filled with tall houses, large window balconies and pointed gables. He knew that decadent lives were lived inside those homes, where fashionable women and smartly-dressed men enjoyed unhurried days inside sprawling rooms, each one decorated with silk carpets, French chandeliers, big fireplaces and fine bedclothes to sleep under.

The Goldstein family lived in a three-story house that was built like an Italian villa. Arno stopped to look up the flight of stone steps that led to the front door. The door itself was wide and painted black and had a brass knocker in the shape of a ram's horn. At the end of the street, a shoe-shiner had set up his stall and was stopping people as they emerged from a nearby park. He called to Arno, who looked down at his footwear, which were creased with lines and scuff-marked all about the rim.

He momentarily thought about getting his shoes cleaned up but instead, to make a point of not caring, he untucked his shirt and ruffled his hair. It was Monika's parents who reminded him that he came from a middlebrow family and that he didn't have any steady wealth. His uneasiness stirred memories of old conversations he used to have with his friends from the youth movement. 'The Jews have managed to maintain their racial purity because they have an instinct for self-preservation. They possess cunning. That's why they are our biggest threat.'

He realised that such views held little truth, as he pushed these thoughts aside. When he rang the bell, Monika's mother answered the door.

'Good afternoon Frau Goldstein. Is Monika in?' he asked.

Frau Goldstein looked at him plainly. She had a broad, attractive face, with bright skin that seemed almost reflective like porcelain. When she spoke, the red lipstick she was wearing expanded and contracted with her lips. 'Please come in Arno.'

She led him through the hall, whose walls were papered with Tyrian purple and the furniture gave off a rich glow of having been polished a thousand times. They both remained silent as he followed her towards the rear of the house.

When they reached the drawing room, he found Monika's father standing at an unlit fireplace with his hands behind his back, rocking on his heels as a clock ticked loudly above the mantelpiece.

Herr Goldstein seemed surprised to see Arno and then proceeded to offer the visitor a seat, which Arno declined. This was only the third time he'd met them. Both times before he'd been presented as Monika's friend from college. He wondered if they had any idea who he *really* was?

'If you've come to see Monika, she's not here,' her father announced. 'She's away on a cultural excursion.'

'I see,' Arno replied. Then the thought: 'Why hasn't she returned?'

'Don't you and Monika take classes together?'

'What?'

'We thought you'd be on the same trip?' her father said.

Arno didn't want to answer. They obviously hadn't seen the photograph which was a good thing, but they didn't know where Monika was either. He sank into his thoughts as his fear started to gnaw at him.

'Tell us, what are you reading?'

'I'm taking a break at the moment. I'm in between subjects,' he said feeling reticent. The truth was he'd completed *Volksschule* and anything he'd learnt since then had come from experiences in the *real* world.

Monika's father was now standing at a side table preparing a drink for himself. 'Ever thought about studying the law?' he asked as he added tiny jets of soda water to his glass of dark brown *Fassbrause*.

'Felix is a lawyer,' the mother confirmed, smiling at her husband.

Felix Goldstein nodded proudly. 'Best decision I ever made Ursula.' He lifted his eyes to the room as if he was saying 'My career paid for all of this,' without actually saying it.

Then all three of them fell silent. Arno was perplexed. He wanted to tell them that there was no drama trip and that Monika was in fact missing. He wanted to shake them up by telling them, and that by doing so, he could win a strange sort of victory – but recognised it would be pointless.

'The law is the ideal meeting point of morality and logic,' Monika's father went on.

Arno sat down and meshed his fingers together as he stared into the blackened fireplace. Then as he listened to Monika's father burden him with advice about a career he would never pursue, a throb of scorn went through him. The law? He'd been operating on the opposite side of the law for years. And what would the law mean when the new politics came into power? Everything was bound to change. Berlin would have no need for the law if the whole order was overturned, at least not the law as Monika's father saw it.

Arno lifted his head and gave a sideways glance out of the window. It was time to leave this house.

'I have to go now. Please, excuse me,' he said, rousing himself.

'Would you like us to give Monika a message? She will be home tomorrow,' Monika's mother said.

'Tell her,' – Arno thought for a second – 'tell her we have much to catch up on.'

As he left the house he knew there was trouble on the horizon. It was time to find out what had happened to Monika and look to his next step.

8

Arno dug his hands into his pockets and began to cross the city on foot. As he walked, he noticed the sound of birds calling from the branches of the horse-chestnut trees that lined the street. That was the sort of district he was in. Trees on the street, expensive motorcars passing by on the road. Where he came from, there were no trees and the birds didn't sing.

The birdsong reminded him of a story Monika once told him. When she was a girl of ten years old, she'd climbed up a beech tree all the way to the top to look at the horizon and dark clouds in the distance. Eventually, she started to lower herself onto the branches to get down again when suddenly several of them snapped. She managed to clutch onto the trunk but grew scared of the drop. Then the weather turned and it began to rain with strikes of lightning. Still, nobody was around to bring her down. After several attempts to climb down, she ended up huddled under the leaf-covered boughs and grew red with cold. She was embarrassed and hoped no one would notice, but at the same time needed *someone* to help her. It wasn't until her father came looking for her and ended up climbing a ladder to coax her down, that she was rescued.

Arno began to think that maybe she'd done something similar, that she'd gone somewhere as a way of disappearing for a short time and then had become stuck or stranded, and for some reason couldn't find her way back again. Maybe she was still waiting for someone to find her and had found a safe place that to her seemed utterly obvious. And yet, he knew thinking like this would drive him mad and so tried to put his speculation to one side.

As he walked on, the afternoon became placid and bright. Up ahead, the street was twinkling with people enjoying the summer air. He saw a young girl in a polka dot dress standing on a street corner selling lemonade from a metal tank strapped to her back. When an open-top tourist bus went by, everyone on board pointed at the little girl and began taking photographs.

Arno went past *Robert's* on the corner where the Kurfürstendamm meets Fasanenstrasse. It was a self-service restaurant just like they have in America. He had more than enough money now to get oysters on salad leaves and a milkshake, or else a julep with an extra shot of bourbon – if only Monika was there to share it!

He walked along the boulevards, crossing Fehrbelliner Platz and along Hohenzollern, north-east in the direction of central Berlin. It nagged at him, this doubt about Monika, as if some sort of concealed truth lay just out of sight. Whatever the effect of the old Nazi photograph upon Monika's feelings about him, he remained determined to find her and tell her that he'd altered his ways since then.

But just as quickly, he changed his mind. He began to think that Monika's disappearance was his fault. Maybe she was repulsed and which made her disappear without warning and never intended to see him again.

He passed beside a line of shops until he came to the end of the block. There were brick walls covered in rows of posters for an election rally that had long since passed.

It was the same poster repeated over and over a hundred times, each poster torn in a different way. The words read *Work, Freedom and Bread!* in striking red lettering.

Just then, a car pulled up in front of him and halted. A rear window began to wind down and behind it appeared a woman smoking a cigarette. It wasn't until he took note of the cream raincoat she was wearing that he recognised her as the very same woman from the train. Yes, it was her, and she was looking directly at him.

'What do you want?' he asked.

She spoke through the window in a strong, confident voice. 'I just wanted to say thank you, again. Thank you for helping us earlier.'

Arno gave a cursory nod of acceptance and proceeded to walk on. The last thing he wanted was to get involved with her again, besides which, his trust in the police was next to nothing.

The motorcar edged around the corner and began to tail him as he walked. He glanced over his shoulder. Unless he broke into a run, it would easily keep pace. But why should he run anyway?

The woman was still teetering through the open door. 'Come and ride with us for a few minutes,' she said. 'We can give you a lift. We'll take you wherever you need to go.'

He walked forward, but the insistence of the car crawling beside him was weakening his resolve. He noticed it was a fine looking car, deep blue in colour, trimmed with silver along its flank. Since when did the police travel in such opulence, he wondered to himself? And then he thought: maybe having a contact in the police would be useful to him? It was possible.

As if this last thought had given him permission, he found himself climbing into the car and onto the back seat. It felt odd – unreal and shady – to be sat there after the events on the train that morning. In the front next to the driver was a plain-clothed policeman.

Arno glanced over to the woman next to him. She was well-dressed and immaculate in her looks. The way she looked, it was hard to believe she had spent the night on the same train as he had.

'Did you arrest that guard on the train? Is he now behind bars?'

'The operation went like clockwork,' she replied. 'Have I introduced myself yet? My name is Hannah Baumer.'

'Where are we going?'

'That depends. Where would you like us to take you?'

Arno peered out of the window and changed the subject. 'That job I did this morning. Was the money also to buy my silence?'

'We don't need to talk about that. Tell me, where have you been just now?'

'Why?'

'You haven't been somewhere in particular?'

He looked over at her. Her expression was solemn yet there was a hint of clemency there too. Could he trust her?

'Arno, isn't it?' she asked. 'Where have you been, Arno?'

He didn't remember telling her his name. He decided to follow his best instincts and deny everything. 'I haven't been anywhere.'

'You don't live around here, do you?'

'What makes you say that?'

'Just a guess. But if you don't live in this district, why would you be here?'

Arno tried not to frown.

'So you haven't been to a house nearby?'

Arno remained poker-faced, as he caught the eye of

the driver in the rear view mirror.

'Perhaps you've been to visit someone?'

'And who would that be?'

'Perhaps you've been to see the Goldstein family?'

'I don't know any Goldsteins.'

'I believe they have a daughter? I think her name is Monika.'

Hearing Monika's name said aloud sent a jolt of trepidation through him. Had the police been following him since the train incident?

'I know you've been to see the Goldsteins. You were there only half an hour ago. Why would you deny it? We can help you.'

'What do you know about Monika?'

'So you do know who I mean? Monika Goldstein?'

'Monika and I are friends. But that's none of your business. Do you know where she is?'

'Friends? I see. That's why you were at her parent's house?'

'Yes.'

'But why? Why would you visit them? Why would you visit them *today*?'

'Well, you seem to know a great deal about my whereabouts! You tell me why I went. Then you can tell me why I'm in this car, talking to you.' Speaking in this way, with a turn of hostility, Arno felt he had regained some advantage. It was no use acting with diffidence in these circumstances. Return a question with another question: that seemed to be the game here.

'Because you are worried about her,' the woman said. 'That's why you got into the car. Well? It's true isn't it?'

'Why would I be concerned about her?'

'Because you don't know where she is. Where is she now? Where is Monika?'

Arno was about to lunge forward and grab Baumer

when the car came to a sudden halt and he became aware there was a pistol being pointed at the side of his head.

'I wouldn't do anything reckless if I were you. You may live to regret it.'

Arno had no choice but to recline back into the seat.

Presently, the car began to pick up speed as it manoeuvred onto a main road that led through the city.

'Where are you taking me?' Arno pressed, recognising the change of pace. 'What have you got to do with Monika?'

Baumer didn't answer.

He sat and made a mental note of where they were travelling. There was no point in trying to get away. The Prussian Police knew something and he had to find out what it was.

9

The conversation with Hannah Baumer fell into silence. Arno watched the city he knew flash by, with its familiar cascade of boulevards with hotels, apartments, cafés and bars, only this time sped up, like one of those movies at the Gloria-Filmpalast. As the car swerved and pummelled through the streets at a headlong rush, he sensed they were trying to rattle him.

'Put this on,' Baumer said, handing him a black band.

Arno stared at her.

'Over your eyes. I suggest you do it now.'

He tied the band across his eyes, placing him in complete darkness. He lost all sense of time and sat tight, waiting for the journey to end. Then the car came to a final stop. He heard the car door next to him open and was lifted out by the arm. The blindfold was stripped off and when his eyes had adjusted to the light, he found himself stood in acres of industrial suburbs.

A large, anonymous building loomed up in front of them. It was a red-brick block, big and stout like a giant chimney, with metal staircases on the outside and small fogged-up windows dotted randomly across the walls. They had driven to a sort of wasteland, where piles of rubble and thickets of brambles lay stretched across patches of wild grass.

Within a few moments, they were out of the car,

crossing the wasteland and climbing one of the metal staircases. At this point, two thickset men appeared from nowhere and followed behind, cutting off any possible exit. The clang of footsteps caused the stairs to vibrate, which accentuated Arno's rising sense of unease as they ascended. He walked behind Baumer, whose high-heeled shoes occasionally caught in the metal grills. He watched as she had to wriggle herself free. He had the sense that she'd done this climb dozens of times before, as she tutted and uprooted herself without looking down to check.

Soon they entered a corridor that tunnelled out to several more doorways. Finally, they arrived in a dimly-lit room that had nothing but a small desk and a narrow bed in the corner. At this point, Arno was told he could lie down if he wanted.

'Sleep for a time, if it suits you,' came a voice, from someone behind him.

'You must be tired after your train journey last night,' said another.

'I'm fine,' Arno replied. 'Let's get on with this.'

He was now accompanied by several new people. He turned around to find that Baumer was gone, replaced by a cohort of young men in brown suits and narrow neckties. They all had fiercely combed hair and pale faces, and were not threatening except perhaps for the way they clung together and swapped looks, as if sharing thoughts between them telepathically.

Arno had never been in circumstances like this before, and now he was here escorted by this army of men, he found the idea of absconding not so easy. Through an archway, they entered a large office. It had a narrow table in the centre surrounded by ten chairs around the edges, and next to it, a smaller rectangular desk with a typewriter. Hung on the far wall was a painting, a landscape with trees and billowing clouds, framed in gold. On the opposite wall hung a large map of Berlin marked with red and green lines. In the far corner, there was a metal-and-glass cubicle with a telephone inside.

Arno was invited to sit at the table and make himself comfortable. Someone handed him a glass of water, which was chilled and jarred down his throat as he drank it. Then from a side door, the man he recognised from the train – that ugly dog with the perfect teeth – entered and sat down opposite him. Only this time he didn't seem so ugly. He'd shaved and combed his hair and looked refreshed, even a touch dapper in a pressed suit and a pair of polished shoes. He had that air of hardiness, an ability possessed by some individuals, to overcome their God-given shortcomings with a fresh coat of panache.

When he sat down opposite Arno, he placed his hands on the tabletop, palms down, and gazed across with hypnotic eyes. It felt like he was about to perform a magic trick.

'What am I doing here?' Arno started up. He felt his courage rise, and began to envisage he could influence the course of things if he could only keep his nerve.

'I'm pleased to see you again,' the police agent said.

'Where's Monika?' Arno snapped back.

'We need to talk to you about *Vendetta*.'

There was that word again, the secret pass that had released him from all manner of trouble earlier that day.

'Vendetta,' the man said again, this time with a grave undertow in his voice.

'It's a codeword,' Arno said, trying to dispute the theatrics. 'Isn't it?'

'Yes, except it's much more than that. It's like an iceberg: there's much more beneath the surface that we can't see.'

Arno sat forward, as if to say, nonchalantly, 'Tell me more.'

'First, a little history lesson, if you will indulge me.'

Arno listened on.

'What do you know of the Munich Putsch?'

That was unexpected. The Munich Putsch? Arno knew most of it. It had been seven or eight years now, but everybody from his world was familiar with the story. Midway through a beer-hall speech by some Bavarian commissioner, a young Adolf Hitler clambered onto the stage, fired a pistol into the air and declared a revolution. It was a rebellion that was eventually stopped in its tracks but not before Hitler and about 3,000 fellow zealots had made a play for half the state offices in Munich, including the police headquarters. Gunfire broke out, killing a few. Hitler was injured and ended up in prison for his troubles. As far as Arno was aware, the putsch was a failure and people looked back on it now with resigned embarrassment.

'Just to refresh your memory, it was an attempt to seize power by right-wing nationalists,' the police agent went on. He sat back, lifting his palms from the table and crossing his arms. 'We think Vendetta may be a codeword for something similar. An underground plot to displace the Reichstag. But this time, they want to make sure it succeeds.'

'So why are you talking to me about it?' Arno asked in disbelief. He felt his presence in the room growing and that all eyes were on him. What the hell did they want with him?

The agent in the pressed suit looked at Arno unconvinced. 'These are your people, aren't they?'

'Who?'

'The fascists.'

'What?' Arno gave a blank shake of the head.

'The National Socialists. The Nazis. They're fascists, are they not?'

'So I understand.'

'And you're a member of their party.'

'Incorrect.'

'We know more about you than you realise. We know you have contacts with this group. We know you attempted to perpetrate' – the agent paused, choosing his words carefully – 'we know you understand the agenda of these people very well.'

'Well, I've never been a member,' Arno said, sitting back in his chair. He fell silent as he began to understand the situation. A few years ago he'd been involved in some anti-Communist activity linked to the Nazi Party. It wasn't official – he'd never joined as a formal member, that was true enough – but he had been firmly connected. He'd helped print and distribute publicity leaflets: fabricated stories about a man being murdered and how the Communists wanted to cover it up. It was, he would admit, an exciting idea at the time. But now his commitment lay in the opposite direction, with different beliefs and his future with Monika.

He looked across at the police agent, wondering what his motives were towards him. What exactly did they know about his previous movements?

The man's next words confirmed it. 'You befriended a man named Erich Ostwald. We know that together you plotted to stir up sentiment against the Communist Party. You produced propaganda material. Isn't that the case?'

Arno felt unable to deny it, only to say that it was all history. 'I'm no longer involved, I've moved on with my life since then,' he said. It was true. He'd lost interest in politics and he'd not seen his accomplice Erich Ostwald in all that time. They had originally crossed paths at a meeting one night. Erich was charismatic and had a philosophic air about him that drew in the younger recruits. They all spoke the same language, about wanting to protect their country and its traditions. It felt like a noble cause at the time. Arno heard Erich Ostwald had gone to Spain since then, leaving everyone – including his pregnant fiancé – in the process. If Arno ever saw him again, he wouldn't be as trusting as he was the first time.

'Moved on with your life?'

'I would never get involved with someone like Erich Ostwald again,' Arno confirmed. 'Let me put it that way.'

'We think Erich Ostwald is back in Germany. And we think he is heavily implicated with the Vendetta movement. Does that news mean anything to you?'

'No. Why should it? I haven't seen him or heard from him since he left.'

'He hasn't tried to contact you?'

'No.'

'Are you sure?'

'Quite sure.'

'Fine. Maybe you could tell me something else. What are your views on politics?'

'Politics? Not much. I've given up following it.'

'What about communism? Don't you have an opinion? What if it came to Germany?'

Arno couldn't help but take the bait. 'Communism? It would more than likely ruin us if we ever adopted it.'

'And what of race? What do you think about people from other backgrounds? Non-Germans? Africans? Jews?'

'I'm not against anybody on such grounds.'

'Is that so? Your history would suggest otherwise.'

'Exactly, it's in the past.'

'Are you not seeing a Jewish girl? How does she fit into your view? Or don't you mind being called a hypocrite?'

'I'm not a hypocrite.'

'Monika? Is she not Jewish?'

'Don't bring her into this.'

'Weren't you against the Jews once?' The policeman tossed a stack of Arno's pamphlets towards him. 'Your writings would propose so.'

The man across the table took a change of tack. He spoke now in more abstract terms, returning to the subject of Vendetta. He told Arno that it was important to understand how any organisation that wanted to threaten the government was also a threat to the greater order. He said that as it grew, such a group would eventually become unstable, with leaders and followers bidding for power, with a hierarchy of internal competition.

'Movements like this become bloated and mistrustful. Individuals grow protective over their gains. They want to extend their territories and win the support of the lesser men. That's when the cracks begin to show. That's when the most foolhardy become vulnerable. This is where you should find your opportunity. Carve a place for yourself, like a weed growing between bricks in the wall.'

'You want me to infiltrate Vendetta?'

'That's right.' The police agent nodded as he began to outline the task. 'We want you to re-join the Party and make a written report back to us.' The agent pointed to a location on a map and explained there was an unofficial letterbox in a wall which would act as a drop-off point. It was grey in colour, knee-height, virtually invisible unless you knew it was there. Any correspondence should be posted in it.

'Report back about what exactly?'

'Of all you see and hear about Vendetta, however inconsequential the details may seem. We think it's a good option for you,' the agent concluded. 'Erich Ostwald is tied to Vendetta. That's the information we have. And you already have a place in their community.'

'Why should I do this?'

'Because we know everything about you. Your activities from three years ago could still bring about charges.'

'I don't see how.'

'Do you want to test me? Or what about your underground trading?' The policeman looked down at his paperwork. 'Chocolate, cigarettes, alcohol. I bet that's just the beginning of it. Am I right?'

Yes, there was some truth in it. Sometimes, when money was tight, Arno had formed part of the transportation network for some of the Ringvereine gangs whose members you could recognise by the style of rings on their fingers and the broken noses they often sported. He'd traded imported alcohol and cigarettes once or twice. Occasionally, he'd taken packages of cocaine across the city.

At this point, the ugly bastard opposite opened up a file and took out an envelope. He slid it across the table in the same arrogant manner he'd slid the money across the table on the train. Inside was a photograph of Arno's sister, Käthe, and her husband Thomas. Beneath that was another photograph, this one of Monika.

Arno was incensed. 'Where the hell did you get these?'

'I'm just letting you know that we have all we need. Say that you will assist us with Vendetta, and we'll ensure all your family is safe.'

Arno stood up, ready to burst across the table. His

anger exploded inside him quickly. He wanted to smash that row of perfect white teeth to the back of his throat. Yet, as he threw a punch at the man opposite, he felt the force of several hands push down on his shoulders, squeezing him back into his chair with a thud.

'The choice is yours,' the man across the table said, pressing his thumb into his lip to find it had been cut. Then, in a turn of phrase that angered Arno even more, he said, 'You're very tense aren't you?'

'I've got every reason to be. This is blackmail.'

'We don't intend to hurt anyone.'

'Where's Monika?' Arno asked angrily as he wiggled in his seat, only to find himself clamped to the spot by the two men on either side of him.

'I don't know. At home? At drama lessons? How would I know?'

'She's disappeared.'

'Has she now?' The policeman's eyes widened. 'You'd better get to work then, hadn't you?'

10

Arno was ushered into another police car and blindfolded again. He travelled the route in silence; the only noises were the muffled sounds of the streets outside. When the car eventually pulled over, he was forcibly ejected onto a grimy roadside, where he rolled over onto his knees and slipped the band off. He found himself on the edges of Potsdamer Platz, where the clocks of the city chimed eight in the evening as he made his way back to his apartment building. It had been raining and the city was slick with water, turning every stone surface into a yellow-grey mirror. As the water sucked at his every step he became aware of the holes in his shoes, feeling his feet turn wet.

On his face, he felt the cool air that follows a downpour. The clouds had passed now, except for a couple of drifting billows that looked like slow-moving battleships slipping out of a harbour. It was dark enough for the windows of cafés and restaurants to begin to glow with yellow lamplight, rectangular portals onto intimate scenes, of lovers and friends out for dinner.

He was standing on the corner of the square, close to the Tiergarten park. Memories of the day's events jostled in his mind like the crowds around him. All he wanted to do was to get drunk. He wanted to escape to a bar somewhere. Maybe he could catch a glimpse of those

African girls dancing to the rhythm of a high-hat. On the street, people were everywhere, returning home from work or going out for the night. They huddled in large clusters around the tram stops, waiting for their transport home, or else they streamed out from the steps of the U-Bahn assessing whether to open or close their umbrellas.

He thought about going to one of his regular haunts, the Hopak Bar, to take his mind off the kaleidoscope of questions. Everyone at the Hopak Bar was a little bit vulgar and a little bit desperate. Still, it came with the territory of city life. It was the only place where aristocrats and paupers were happy to rub shoulders. Perhaps they thought they might swap places one day. The bar always had a huge bowl of pink punch at the entrance, with lemons swimming around on top, and for a few coins you could get a ladle of it decanted into a glass with a paper straw. It was a matter of chance if you got drunk on it or not, depending on the night of the week and which bar-tender had made up the bowl.

He thought about Monika. The question of where she was seemed desperately out of reach. Did the police really know something or was it a bluff? He was exhausted and confused, and the tangle of uncertainty about her remained untamed.

Yet, there was still a part of him that expected her to turn up at any minute. Even after the grave conversation he'd had with the police agent, he still trusted Monika to find her way home. He believed innately that she would shake off whatever forces or bad decisions had overtaken her, and at any moment, he would see her face smiling at him again.

The thought stayed with him through the night. He decided against the Hopak Bar and went directly home instead. He ate beans and bread for dinner and drank two bottles of beer.

As he sat on the floor with his back against a wall, he went over the strange exchange with the police. Just because they'd presented him with some truths about his past didn't mean he had to consent to them. He could have flatly denied it, asserted himself by keeping his mouth shut. What could they have done if he'd remained mute like that? Torture it out of him? They needed him to admit his history, and by letting them claw it from him he'd given them the power they needed to blackmail him. It didn't really matter to them where his beliefs stood now, they were adamant about using his prior attachment to the Nazis as a way to force him into their operation. Namely Vendetta.

Then they had revealed those photographs of Monika and his sister, which caught him off guard. The photographs had put him under pressure and backed him into a corner. No wonder he leapt across the table to throttle the wretched policeman. Using his closest and dearest as pawns was a dirty game.

He took another mouthful of beer and listened to the sound of fire brigade sirens bawling down the street. He didn't know what would happen next. The police had told him he would find out how his assignment would proceed soon enough. All he could do was wait and grapple with the unknown. He was involved in Vendetta now. The word was a mystery, whispered rumours of more political agendas and the bad news that was Erich Ostwald – at least that was the story the police had given.

Meanwhile, Monika was still out there somewhere and he needed to do all he could to get her back. If appearing to act on behalf of the police meant he was one step closer to finding her, then that was what he would have to do. He had no allegiance to them; he would use them just as they were using him. He decided, he needed to contact his sister and find out if she'd heard anything. Had the police spoken with her or tried to intimidate her too? Erich had been friends with her and in particular her husband – any involvement with him could land them in deep water.

He went to bed and took a mental image of Monika with him. Even in the morning it was still there. He couldn't shake off the idea that she had spent the night alone and vulnerable somewhere, just waiting for him to find her. He knew his feelings were not just about her beauty and good grace, nor just about their time in the hotel room together, but were connected to something more fundamental than that. He knew he loved her. If he saw her right now, he wouldn't hesitate to tell her how he felt. Then he realised, what angst it was, to want to say 'I love you' to someone who isn't with you and whom you may never see again.

11

Café Bauer was a Viennese-style coffee house on Friedrichstrasse. It had red velvet chairs and golden columns that reached up to a carved, swirling ceiling. The bust of a Greek youth stood in a scalloped alcove surrounded by large mirrors along the high walls that gave the impression of a room two or three times its actual size. The whole establishment hummed with the clinking of cutlery and polite chit-chat, along with the faint sound of a quartet playing Mozart in some hidden corner.

Arno was there to meet his sister, Käthe. After his meeting with the police, he wanted to check she was unharmed and if she might know something too.

Käthe was eight years older than Arno and had, in his opinion, easily adopted the good life that Berlin made available to some. She and her new husband, Thomas, lived in an upmarket apartment on the Kurfürstendamm not far from Berlin Zoo. They dressed well, socialised often, took picnics to the lakes at Wannsee and tried their hand at sailing. Of course, they were in love. They had that way about them that newly married couples often do: somewhat in awe of one another, and almost oblivious to everyone else.

Arno passed through a heavy green curtain that opened out onto the main seating area, and as he did, he was immediately accosted by the head waiter. He felt a hand on his elbow as the tight-lipped waiter tried to lead him back towards the exit. Arno, being amused, thought it was his bent-up shoes and ragged shirt collar that marked him out as the opposite of well-to-do folk.

He protested, but the waiter, who was made-up with pale silvery cheeks, only gripped his arm more firmly, saying, 'Don't make me call the kitchen boys, they won't be so gentle.'

Fortunately, Käthe and Thomas were just coming through the green drapes as Arno and the waiter began to argue. And being as Thomas had only two years before come into a great deal of money, inherited from a benefactor whom everyone presumed penniless, their arrival turned everything on its head. The waiter's bright blue eyes widened and he began to nervously finger the white napkin in his breast pocket. 'Come, come,' he now muttered, leading the group of three back into the café, between the tables and towards a favoured spot beneath the tall windows. Käthe tipped the waiter in a cool, almost invisible gesture, and he left them to settle around the marble-top table.

'It's been a long time,' Thomas was the first to say as they sat down. 'How have you been, Arno? Not in any trouble I hope,' he said as he winked.

Arno slouched back in his chair. He didn't like Thomas' directness – nor his astuteness. He'd never been sure of his sister's choice of husband. The man was too cautious for Arno's tastes, one of those people who seemed to know the right and wrong of everything. In Thomas, Arno saw an inverted image of himself. Additionally, because Thomas was so unconscionably wealthy.

'In trouble? Me?' Arno said innocently. He began scratching the tabletop with his fingernail.

'Are you working at the moment?' Käthe asked.

'I've got plenty of options,' he replied.

Thomas himself was pleased to be there. Arno was someone he admired, though he tended to keep that opinion to himself. Arno was carefree and sometimes foolhardy – and he wished he could be more like that sometimes.

'Something will turn up,' Thomas said, not meaning to sound as condescending as he did. 'You'll be fine.'

Arno then pretended to yawn, to show he didn't give a damn. Then out of the blue, he said, 'Have the police been in contact with you?' He'd meant to say it with concern for his sister but it seemed to come out as a threat.

'No, why would they have been?' Thomas asked, alarmed.

'You might be interested to know, I've heard that Erich Ostwald is back in the country. In fact, he's back in Berlin by all accounts. The police are rather attentive to him apparently.'

He watched as Käthe and Thomas passed glances between each other.

'Where did you hear that?' his sister asked.

Arno hadn't thought through his disclosure and wasn't sure now how much he should reveal. It suddenly occurred to him that being covert in this way indicated that his work for the police had already begun.

'He wrote to me,' he lied.

'Erich wrote to you?' Thomas said. Both he and Käthe moved forward a fraction.

'I got a letter from him two days ago. That's what I wanted to tell you. He wrote to me, mentioning he was coming back to Berlin. He said something about wanting to get behind the movement again.'

'The last I heard, Erich Ostwald was in Spain,'

Thomas said. He was trying his best to keep to a matter-of-fact poise. Hearing Erich's name again made him feel instinctively ambiguous.

'Have you got the letter with you?' Käthe asked. 'Can we see it?'

'No, I left it at home.'

'You should have brought it with you.'

'I'm telling you what was in it. What's the difference?'

'What else?' Thomas pressed him. 'What else did it say?'

Arno watched as Thomas fell silent into his own thoughts. The two of them – Erich and Thomas – had been old friends once, that is until the whole anti-Communist stunt put a wedge between them. Thomas had been a pawn in Erich's game back then. He'd wanted Thomas to play a role in the plot, but Thomas didn't fall into line. Now the friendship had faded to nothing.

'I wonder if he'll have the gall to try to find me?' Thomas said, turning to Käthe. There was both hope and curiosity in his tone. He knew that his old friend had spent the last two years in Spain. Beyond that, any other details were hazy. The letters Erich wrote to his fiancé said he'd been in the city of Zaragoza, where he'd apparently joined a military academy. He wrote of *'pressures growing in America'* and *'market troubles that could destroy our great country if we don't protect it.'*

Erich's words had proved prophetic. Since then, the stock markets in the U.S. had nose-dived and the waves that came rippling over the Atlantic were like great tsunamis. Factories closed one after another. Government workers were laid-off in droves. You could hardly walk into a shop without being accosted by a malnourished beggar.

All these were signs that Berlin was morphing into a more dangerous city. The sight of columns of men marching to the clash of cymbals or singing *Raise the Flag* was all too common. Thomas himself had run into one such gang on the Leipzigerstrasse one night, when a bunch of thugs began smashing the windows of Jewish shops and intimidating anyone passing by. He had crossed the street to avoid the melee, but a couple of the brown-shirted roughs split from the crowd and followed him. They waved leaflets in his face; when he refused to take one, they grabbed him beneath the arms and began stuffing fistfuls of paper into his coat. One of them punched his shoulder, then left him in the road by pushing him onto the ground. Thomas felt like he got off lightly.

And now! Was Erich Ostwald really back in Berlin to join the fray? Could he be only a step away? The idea that he might run into him on any street corner concerned him far more than a group of sabre-rattling bullies.

'I sincerely hope he doesn't try to find you,' Käthe replied.

'He doesn't know where we live, so that reduces the chances, by a little anyway.'

'Not unless Arno has told him.' She looked at her brother. 'Have you told him where we live?'

'No, I haven't said anything. There was no address to reply to, anyway.'

'Did it say anything else? This letter? Why exactly was he writing to you?'

Arno stumbled through his thoughts. 'I don't know. He was letting me know, I suppose, that he's back in Germany.'

'Does he want you to do something for him? What was that part about getting behind the movement again?

What did he mean?'

'You know, the Nazis. They plan to overturn the current situation. There are a lot of people who hate the system as it stands.' As he spoke, Arno sensed he was drawing their attention. 'In fact, there are lots of people who hate Berlin and the direction it's taking. They think they've suffered enough. The Nazis intend to do something about it.'

At this point, the waiter returned to the table to take their order. Knowing Thomas would pay, Arno had no hesitation in ordering a double cognac with ice, which was more or less the most costly thing on the menu. Thomas ordered a coffee; Käthe a sweet wine.

'Will you be eating?' the waiter asked.

'Liver and mushroom pâté,' Arno said quickly. The other two shook their heads.

'Please tell me you're not still involved,' Käthe said. 'I mean, with all that hateful politics?'

'It's all around us. It would be irresponsible not to be involved.'

'I thought you'd disentangled yourself from all that business? The way you're talking, it sounds like you could become implicated in their activities again.'

'Me? Not any more. I wouldn't be telling you about Erich's letter if I was, would I?'

'I suppose not.'

'How do you know the police are interested in his return?' Thomas asked.

'Erich mentioned it in his letter.'

Käthe and Thomas said nothing. Arno looked about him, around Café Bauer and its strange, ornate decoration. His eyes landed on a nearby table of four men in military uniform. They were chatting and smoking, laughing at a joke one of them had made. Arno wondered which side they were on. He couldn't see their badges. Freikorps were everywhere around the city, many of them old army veterans who needed something to fill the void. Arno began to wonder if he'd been born a few years earlier and had fought in the war, whether he'd be a member of one of these private armies too.

One of the men, he noticed, had a pistol in his belt. That caught Arno's attention. He had a slim face, with wide eyes and short, cropped hair swept back from a high forehead. He roared with laughter long after the other men had finished being amused.

Then Arno's mind turned back to the day before with the police agent. He didn't know how his assignment would unfold. But now, sat with his sister and her husband in this café, he felt a wave of responsibility roll over him – a mission that was all his own. It didn't matter that he couldn't tell them about it. And seeing the four military men sat there, the way they laughed and looked so unshakable – he couldn't help look for the pistols hanging from all the other belts too – they reminded him how it was better to be involved in *some* way rather than standing on the sidelines watching on, merely complaining and ignorant.

'What are you looking at?' Käthe asked him. 'You shouldn't stare.'

'Nothing,' Arno said back conceitedly. A short time later, a plate of creamy pâté with toasted bread and some salad leaves was placed on the table in front of him, and with it a cut-glass tumbler of cognac on ice. Through mouthfuls of food, he said assuredly, 'If Erich Ostwald attempts to make contact with you, you must tell me.'

'Why?'

'Because I have a score to settle with him. I would have landed in deep water, just like Thomas, if his propaganda stunt worked. I want to tell him I have my own beliefs now. Besides, I wouldn't have met Monika either if I still thought like him.' Arno knew he was laying it on thick, but it was the only way he could get Käthe and Thomas to agree.

'If it closes the matter for you, then fine.'

'How's your girlfriend?' Thomas asked.

'I haven't seen Monika for days. We went away for a weekend but we parted company.'

'Oh Arno!' Käthe said. 'Why? What did you do *this* time?'

'What makes you think I did anything?'

'Talk to her. Make things better again.' Käthe took her husband's hand and gave it a squeeze, as if to remember something private between them.

'I can't. I don't know where she is.'

'Go to her home. She lives with her parents doesn't she? Find her and talk to her. Or perhaps she is staying with friends.'

Arno sat back and folded his arms. 'Yes, it's possible she's with friends.' He didn't want to admit that something much worse may have happened. His sister would blame him; he knew the way her mind worked.

The party of three stayed on at the café for another half an hour. They talked mostly about Käthe and Thomas' plans to renovate their apartment, but Arno's attention was elsewhere. He was still drawn to the table of men in uniforms and to the man with the high forehead in particular. He had a noble way about him and a dauntless demeanour along with it. As the group finished their drinks, the man stood and adjusted the red band on his left arm. When he had flattened it out, Arno could see the black hooked-cross symbol of the Nazi Party set against a white circle. The four men pulled on their circular caps and wandered off to the door. Arno's eyes watched as a pulse of anticipation ran through him, knowing he would be back among their number soon.

12

After Café Bauer, Arno walked the city alone. The meeting with his sister and her husband had put him in a better position. It was clear the police hadn't been in touch with either of them. His sister was safe, for now at least, but he'd done nothing to prepare her for any dangers ahead. How could he? He wasn't fully aware of the situation himself.

As he walked, he found himself returning to the quarters of the city where Erich Ostwald used to take him, as if retracing the steps of his old mentor. He went to the medieval Altberlin area and then onto Scheunenviertel where, several years earlier, they'd met at a tavern and spent time hatching plans for their propaganda pamphlets. Later he went to Erich's old apartment building near the Tiergarten. He remembered being inside the apartment and looking out through the tall windows over the park from an interior that was luxuriously furnished. They were eye-opening times. He wondered what had happened to all those auspicious objects.

Then, all of a sudden – though he couldn't believe his eyes – he thought he saw the man himself. Across the road, no more than twenty paces away. The silhouette was the same, the bearing, the gait, that loose turn of stride.

Arno was taken aback. It seemed too implausible, that on this very day he should see Erich Ostwald. But then, it would be just like Erich to organise such a coincidence. Perhaps it wasn't a chance occurrence at all but an orchestrated meeting? The figure came and went in an instant. Something told Arno to follow, like that flash of recognition where the mind's instinct is a beat ahead of the conscious thought.

The figure moved towards a crowd and was consumed by a breaking wave of people. The crowd was in fact a long line of men queuing to buy sausages from a street vendor. Arno hunted among the straggling queue for the figure that had disappeared amongst it. A tram vibrated by as a stream of commuters flooded the square ahead of him from a nearby underground station. And then a fluttering panic of doves turned the sky into a percussion of rattling wings.

Arno caught sight of the figure again, just as it passed beneath the archway of a shopping arcade. He moved faster towards the silhouette. A line of newspaper sellers with the daily editions pegged to their chests formed a sort of barricade along the roadside; an overweight man with a walking cane was browsing the headlines. Arno jumped to one side and moved past the fat gentleman. He paced across the square before waiting for a line of motorcars to go by. He momentarily hid behind an advertising column, then moved on, all the time keeping his eyes on the strolling man ahead of him.

The figure never looked back, never broke his stride nor made any overt suggestion of knowing he was being followed. And yet, with every glimpse he snatched, Arno felt more and more certain that it was his old accomplice. The dark auburn hair was just as he remembered, and the light-coloured casual suit with long flapping pockets was just Erich's style.

Arno passed beneath an overhead train line and saw the man turn into a side street. The narrow alley had uneven cobbles underfoot and damp walls whose plaster rendering was falling off. There was a cripple selling vegetables from a wooden cart and four cats sleeping together in a ring.

Finally, Arno saw the figure glance over his shoulder. Their eyes connected for just a moment. It was long enough: it was undoubtedly Erich. There was no mistaking it. Yet, just as Arno was about to call out, expecting Erich to stop and allow him to catch up, the figure turned away and at twice the pace went through a slender archway under a wall.

The archway led into a cemetery. There were gravestones and trees. The man moved deftly between the stones, even appearing to glide among them, persuading Arno to follow in a strange type of surrender. It felt less like following now and more like a sort of game, where the only rule was to retain a certain distance – neither too close nor too far away.

Then, as they reached a leafy corner of the burial ground, where a deep-green oak tree overhung and made shadows as dark as its boughs, Erich disappeared. By the time Arno reached the same opening, Erich was no longer in sight.

Arno felt his heart racing, not just from the chase but because he knew something fundamental had changed in the last few minutes.

He went home and spent the rest of the afternoon fixated by the memory of the pursuit. The rumours of Erich Ostwald were true. He was back in Berlin. And Arno knew he had to get closer to him.

He promptly fell asleep. It was a sleep that could have gone on for hours, but it was abruptly interrupted by a sharp banging on his attic hatch. When he didn't rush to answer, the knocking came again, swiftly, more impatiently this time. He shuffled off his bed and went to the hatch. When he lifted it back, he found a man with small ears and wide hazel-coloured eyes peering up at him.

The man handed Arno a manila folder.

'What is it?'

'It's your assignment.'

Arno took it.

The man blinked. Then, with a perfunctory glance, he moved to the staircase. Before he descended, he looked over his shoulder and said, 'You will begin tomorrow. Don't be late.'

PART II – MONIKA

13

Three days earlier, Monika Goldstein woke up contented. She was lying in a hotel bed with Arno sleeping beside her. As she laid her head on his chest she felt the strong, generous oscillation of his heartbeat. Glancing across the bedsheets, she tried to distinguish between the landscape of mounds and ridges, the cotton swells of their overlapping bodies.

Then sometime around seven in the morning, she heard footsteps outside the locked door. Every so often there were more footsteps. She guessed they belonged to the other guests going to breakfast or to the housekeeping staff. The feeling of being in an unfamiliar room like this intrigued her, for she seldom had the opportunity to stay overnight away from home.

The hotel room was pretty and quaint, the sort of room her parents would appreciate. It was only the second time she'd ever stayed in a hotel. The first was in Paris when her parents decided – uncharacteristically – to celebrate her sixteenth birthday in style. That hotel room was wood-panelled and very small. This one was much larger, had a high ceiling and long, uneven walls. It accommodated their few belongings easily, as if they were hardly present at all.

The room had its own bathroom too. That in itself

was remarkable. In Berlin, she doubted they would get a single bed with a shared washbasin down the hall for the same money. But in this archaic little town, with its old clock tower scheduled to perform a mechanical show every hour, they had managed to rent this suite for the weekend.

Turning her head to look at Arno, she felt a tender affection for his sleeping face, firm and still in the warm atmosphere of the room. Every so often she wondered what a future with him would look like. His prospects didn't amount to much, according to her parents. Most of all, he wasn't Jewish. That was probably the most insurmountable issue. But tradition wasn't everything, and besides, in her faith it was the woman who naturally passed the lineage onto any children…

She dismissed the thought. To think like that bored her immediately. Life wasn't about judging people's religions or their career prospects, it was about carving your own path in pursuit of your flow of happiness. Right now she felt free here in this hotel room. If it wasn't for Arno, she wouldn't be away on this adventure. She would be at home instead, waking up in her bedroom, listening to her parents moving around downstairs like two chess pieces in a game that had been going on for years, confined to her room with only her writing desk and candlesticks for company.

She put her head on the pillow and started to doze. Before she knew it, she woke to the caress of Arno's hand on her thigh. For a minute she played along as his fingers made a flirtatious dance along her leg. Then she slipped out of bed to cross the room into the bathroom. The stone floor was warm beneath her feet from the rays of the morning sun.

After five minutes, she heard knocking on the door. She called to Arno but there was no response from him.

She peeked into the bedroom and saw that the bed was empty and he wasn't in the room. A second knock came. There was no spyhole in the door, so she couldn't see who was on the other side. She decided it was probably one of the hotel maids, so she wrapped a nightgown around her shoulders and went to answer it. As she eased back the door, she was suddenly aware that it might be her parents on the other side. Had they discovered her whereabouts and now come to escort her home?

To her relief, she saw the face of a woman. A pretty woman in a cream raincoat. She was stood in the corridor holding a small attaché case to her chest.

'It's Monika isn't it?' the woman inquired, smiling, half-whispering. She gently tucked a strand of hair behind one ear.

'Yes.'

'Monika Goldstein?'

'Who are you?'

'Do you have a moment to talk?'

Monika didn't know how or what to answer.

The woman continued in her hushed voice. 'Please don't be alarmed. I'm here as a friend. I have some information you may wish to see, if I can take a few minutes of your time?'

'What's this about? It's very early.' Monika glanced behind her expecting Arno to be there. Where was he?

'I'm sorry if I seem impertinent. Only, there is some urgency in what I have to tell you – it's a delicate matter.'

'What is it?'

'Shall we go somewhere more discreet?'

Monika turned away from the woman, feeling confused. 'Just give me a moment.' She went back inside the room and quickly threaded herself into some clothes. She thought about brushing her hair. Instead, she brushed her teeth and put her hair into a bun.

Together they walked the length of the hotel corridor in silence. 'Am I in trouble?' Monika asked as they reached the reception hall.

'Not at all,' the woman said assuredly. 'This is about your safety.' When she smiled, her face seemed to expand with warmth. Monika noticed how pristine the woman was and how graceful her gestures were. She couldn't think what she would want with her.

They went to an alcove in the far corner where there was a faded tapestry on the wall and an iron candelabra hanging from the ceiling. They sat opposite each other, on two benches on either side of a heavyset wooden table.

'Let me tell you what this is about,' the woman said. 'The man you are with. His name is Arno Hiller, is it not?'

Monika's eyes widened. 'Yes, why do you ask?'

'How much do you know about him?'

Monika said nothing. She was trying to pin down the exact thrust of the question. 'Enough,' she said vaguely. 'Actually, we're well acquainted,' she added.

'The thing is, we're worried about you.'

Monika was about to respond when she noticed a man arriving into the reception hall. He was coming directly towards them. She noticed the black suit he was wearing, how it didn't seem to fit him very well, sagging at the sleeves and shiny over the knees. Without saying anything, the man manoeuvred onto the bench beside the woman. He had deep set eyes and cheeks that were lumpy and covered in stubble. By contrast with her, he was no more beautiful than a sack of potatoes.

Without introducing himself, he took the lead in the conversation. 'Arno Hiller is known to us as an agitator. Do you understand what I mean by that?'

Monika refused to answer. With two of them now sitting in front of her, she suddenly felt intimidated in a way she hadn't only seconds before. But in a split second, the feeling evaporated. 'You'll have to excuse me but you must have him mixed up with someone else.' Then she turned to the woman. 'This is the reason you wanted to talk to me?'

'Let me explain,' the man went on, 'Arno Hiller has a propensity to generate trouble. Political trouble. He has connections with people who are violent and corrupt. They are ambitious too.'

Monika frowned. 'Who are you?'

'Our concern is for you, Monika,' the woman responded, sensing the change of atmosphere.

'How do you know my name? Or that we were here?'

The man continued, 'Arno Hiller is a threat to your safety.'

'It isn't true,' Monika replied.

He handed over a sheet of paper. Monika held it in her fingers and stared at it for a long time. Even though it was early in the morning, her mind was razor-sharp. She laid the paper on the table, perplexed by why they would want to show it to her.

'I don't believe this has got anything to do with Arno or me,' she said. She looked down again at the piece of paper. No matter how nervous she felt reading the words printed on the page, she felt on safe territory. At this, a tiny satisfaction began to rise inside her.

'Why do you say that?' the woman asked.

'I know Arno. He wouldn't be involved in anything like this.'

'This is no mistake,' the man said gravely. 'Do you know what you're looking at?'

'This is Nazi publicity, isn't it?' A girl from her background, with her education, had been taught to know these things and to speak plainly about them.

'Is that so?' the woman questioned.

'Nazi. Isn't that what people call them? Or is it Sozi now?' She could feel her voice verging towards the impertinent. She didn't mind sounding derogatory.

'You mean the National Socialists' Party?' the woman said.

'Yes. But it's propaganda, isn't it? I'm right, aren't I? I know I'm right.' She looked down again at the pamphlet and allowed herself to become acquainted with its contents. It was anti-Communist and anti-Jewish all at the same time. Cruel, disgusting stuff. 'Don't let the monsters take over!' it read. The more she looked at it, the more of a joke it seemed.

'Yes, it's propaganda. The important thing for you to know is that he made that pamphlet. Your boyfriend. That very pamphlet you are holding, he made that with his own hands.'

'I don't believe you.'

'He had a manual printing press to do the job.'

Monika looked away and paused. She'd once seen a printing machine in Arno's attic rooms. He'd said he was looking after it for an old colleague, who'd moved away and showed no signs of reclaiming it.

'Are you beginning to understand why we came to talk to you?' the woman asked.

'No,' Monika responded. Her assuredness was undimmed. She didn't want to listen to their reasonings. Her parents had taught her about material like this. It scared her, but she knew Arno couldn't be mixed up in anything like this.

'Arno Hiller was once involved in a plot to stir up dissent against enemies of the National Socialists' Party.' For the first time, the woman's voice carried a harsher quality. 'In other words, agitation against Jews, Catholics and Communists alike.'

'And we have reason to believe,' the man continued, 'that he is presently engaged in a plot to overthrow the government, most likely using violent means to achieve his goals.'

Monika listened. Part of her wanted to laugh. She could hear every word they were saying with absolute clarity, and they sounded absurd. At first, the idea simply bounced off her. Arno was not like that. She knew how people could be; she was not naive to the possibilities of human hatred, but Arno wasn't that sort of person. She was too wary to let him fool her like that.

'Why should I believe you?' she asked.

The woman took out a booklet from her bag and held it up. It contained her identity papers. Her name was Hannah Baumer. Her papers stated that she worked for the Prussian Police.

'We want to keep you safe. That's our only motivation.'

Monika started to feel disillusioned by the people sat opposite her. They weren't making her feel safe. Quite the opposite. They had lured her away from her room and were filling her head with stories. Yet, she began to feel her resolve crack as she considered there was the slimmest chance that what they were saying could be true. There was plenty she didn't know about Arno, she had to admit that. And with the admission, she felt a bolt of fear suddenly rise inside her chest. A glimpse of darkest doubt. She wished at this moment that Arno would turn up and explain everything, but he didn't.

'No, you have no proof,' she said shaking her head. She rose from the bench, attempting to step away. 'There's no truth in what you are saying. I must go now.'

'Wait.' It was at this point that the man brought out a photograph. He placed it onto the table very deliberately, and with a swivel of his fingers, turned it around to face her. She sat back down as he slid the photo across the table right beneath her gaze. Her heart began to beat hard. It was, she realised to her shock and dismay, their winning hand. The photo showed Arno stood alongside a group of Nazi compatriots. It was unmistakably him, a few years younger than he was now, but undoubtedly the same Arno she had shared a bed with the night before. An object like this could not be invented, nor its meaning refuted.

'No. Not Arno – how could he?' she thought to herself. It was a mighty blow. The hostile thoughts she had towards the man and woman opposite seemed to cool and solidify. There was no point in fighting them now. She had been betrayed. She took a deep breath, as a sense of scorn rose within her. 'You must be tracking Arno's movements?' she stammered. 'Spying on him? Is that right? Would it be simpler if I was out of the picture?'

As she said this, she saw the two strangers on the other side of the table visibly relax. They were happy to concede to Monika's assessment if it meant they might win the wider argument. For a fraction of a second, she thought she might cry, but she contained it. Her only thought now was to get herself out of this business.

'We want to take you back to Berlin. We have a car waiting outside right now.'

'Back to my parents? No, they mustn't find out where I've been.'

'Don't worry. We have a room for you to stay in tonight, if you want. You'll be comfortable there. You can remain there for as long as you need in fact. Until things have settled down.'

Monika felt backed into a corner. 'Fine. One night. I'll stay there for one night, until I can go home.' As she relented, she thought to herself there was still a part of her that wanted to trust Arno. She got up from the table.

'Where are you going?' Baumer asked.

'If I have to leave, I need to get my things.'

'No. There's no time to go back to the room. You must come now.'

'I'm not dressed properly.'

'Someone will collect those for you later.'

Monika felt a tear trickle down her cheek. She recognised deep down she couldn't face the room upstairs again.

'It's better this way. You must come now,' the woman said putting her arm around her. 'It's the best choice.'

14

The clothes they gave her in place of her own were plain and simple. Except, that is, for a black and white pin-striped scarf that felt oddly opulent and silky. Along with the clothes, they gave her a sweet spongecake to eat for breakfast, which she turned over in her fingers and took tiny nibbles from. She wasn't feeling hungry.

She was travelling in an unfamiliar car, alone but for the driver who had a huge black moustache and wore a stiff cap, who said absolutely nothing. Their eyes met every so often in the small rear-view mirror; his green pupils stared at her and made no expression whatsoever.

Above all, she felt foolish and disconcerted. What had transpired this weekend felt utterly surreal. She never expected to be sent back to Berlin, like she was a return-to-sender package! She sat back in her seat and watched the countryside glide by. They passed small holdings and allotments, farms and factories, distant villages and dense forests.

She began to wonder if it was a mistake to leave Arno like that. Maybe she should have heard him out? It felt impossible to analyse everything she'd been told and her head began to spin with the thought that she'd been deceived – by *someone*. Seeing Arno dressed as a fascist was too much. He was no longer the same boy she'd eaten with and laughed with the night before, whom she'd spent the morning gazing at.

She trusted she would be back in her family home soon enough. She could think more objectively then. Her parents were expecting her tomorrow. Return too soon and they'd have too many questions: What happened? Did the drama excursion not suit you? Did someone say something inappropriate to you? Did someone *do* something inappropriate to you?

It was easier this way, she thought. Easier to stay wherever these lawful people had set aside for her. She hoped it would be comfortable. The police would look after her, wouldn't they? She hoped wherever they were taking her would have some privacy and that the food would be suitable.

Outside, the road signs began to read *Berlin*, which was a relief. The man and woman who had put her into the car had not come with her. They'd stayed back in the village and let her travel alone with the driver in the cap. Why was he so silent? Perhaps he had no authority to speak, she thought. Was that how these people worked, according to rules and hierarchy, permission to talk or else stay quiet?

After another hour, she was thankful to see the silhouette of her home city coming into view. The car kept to the road straight into Berlin. She was nearly restored. Yet she still had tears to be shed. Her encounter with the police had cast doubts over Arno. How could a photograph be disproved? Her trip with him had been repudiated and the love she had to offer censored, denied, turned around and sent home. She felt hurt, bitter and conflicted to the very centre of her being.

The car stopped. She got out and found herself on a dusty road lined with brick warehouses, many of which had smashed or boarded-up windows. There was a gravel yard with a pile of old motorcar tyres lying in a heap, like a bunch of black grapes left to rot in the heat. She was led into a building which she took to be the police safehouse. It had a brass door handle the shape of a lion's head with its long tongue sticking out.

She was shown into a room with a double bed and embroidered linen. There was a large chest of drawers with a green vase on top. She was pleased to see a lamp in the corner set on a table next to the bed. She thought she would ask for a book to read – she would need something to pass the time and distract her. Of course, the question was still stirring: how could Arno deceive her like that?

There was a woman with her now. She was small and old. She seemed to be in charge of the room and perhaps other rooms like it in the building. Do you work for the police too? Monika wanted to ask. But it seemed naive to do so, so she stayed quiet.

Could she have a drink? That was a question she did ask. And something to eat? She was hungry now. She'd eaten the sweet cake almost without noticing. The old lady obliged and brought her a glass of water. Monika sat on the edge of the bed and drank three-quarters of the glass in gulps. Shortly after, the old woman hobbled out of the room and came back with a bowl of vegetable soup and a thick piece of bread on a tray, which she left on the bedside table and told Monika to eat while it was still hot. Then, turning, she pointed to a narrow door in the wall which Monika had assumed was a wardrobe. 'Toilet,' she said, and promptly left the room.

As Monika watched her leave, she noticed the woman lock the door behind her.

Monika got up from the bed, went to the door and shook the handle. She crouched down and could see the key was in the lock. At first, she thought it was for her own protection: except that couldn't be right. The key was on the outside. Anyone could turn it. The only person who couldn't was her.

She sat back down on the bed and thought about eating the soup. It looked thick and flavoursome. Steam rose from its surface like a dancing spirit and made the window above mist up. Only now, since she'd noticed the locked door, she'd lost her appetite. She went back to the door and knocked on it. When no one came, she called out and knocked louder. Eventually, the key turned and the door opened gently.

'What is it?' the old woman asked. She spoke softly. She had a kindly sort of face. Monika noticed that one of her eyes had clouded over to a blue-grey fog and was probably blind. It was like she had the moon inside her eye.

'Why am I locked in?'

'We have to lock all the doors,' the woman said. 'That's the rule for everyone.'

'But why?'

The old woman came inside and urged Monika to sit down beside her. She must have weighed next-to-nothing as the bed hardly moved under her weight.

'The locks on the doors are to keep everyone in their rooms,' she said, as if to explain without actually saying very much.

Monika considered, that if this was a boarding house there could be all sorts of other people staying here – misfits, drifters, low-lives – in which case she might be pleased to be locked in behind a door. Then she had a second thought. 'But if I agreed to come here, why should I be locked inside?' Monika said.

The old lady scratched the tip of her nose. Her fingers were thin and long, like tree twigs. 'You may feel that way today,' she said, 'but tomorrow you may feel differently.'

Monika had the sense that the old woman was trying her best to be honest but was unable – for whatever reason – to be completely truthful.

'What is your name?' Monika asked.

The woman's face lit up a little at the question. 'My name is Frau Lange.'

'Do you work here?'

'Yes, of course. I'm here to look after you. I look after everybody here. I'll bring you a meal later, and in the morning, a wash-basin and some breakfast.'

It was only then that Monika took note of Frau Lange's comment from a minute before. 'What did you mean, that I may feel differently tomorrow? I'll be going home tomorrow.'

Frau Lange sighed, as she lifted herself up from the bed and walked slowly to the door without saying another word.

Monika called after her. 'I can't stay here any longer than that.'

The old woman turned and smiled, still saying nothing, only pointing to the soup on the table. Then she left the room and locked the door behind her again. Monika lifted her feet up and lay back on the bed, aware that the old lady had evaded her comment about leaving tomorrow.

She put her head against the pillow and thought about her parents. She hadn't yet decided what she would tell them, whether to be absolutely frank with them or a little poetic with the truth. Since her father was a lawyer, he was bound to have something to say about the manner in which the police had treated her – if she chose to divulge the details.

Herr Goldstein had started his own private practice in Berlin twelve years ago and was something of a force in the community. Since Jewish people had been all but excluded from judiciary and civil service roles, setting up on his own like that was the only choice available to him. Younger lawyers looked up to him for his forthrightness. The question was more or less the same for them all: how to prosper against the grain. Many Jewish lawyers played down their background in order to fit in; some even chose to be baptised. However, Monika's father did it by sheer force of will, which had brought him local renown.

Remembering her father like this gave her an assured feeling. He would guarantee her safety, she knew that with certainty. And with these thoughts, she was soon fast asleep.

When she awoke some hours later, she found Frau Lange in the doorway carrying a folded linen cloth beneath her arm. Monika propped herself up on her elbows and watched from the bed. The old lady went to the bedside table, removed the lamp from it and pulled the table to the middle of the floor. She draped the cloth over the table, then from a pocket in her apron took out a knife and fork and arranged them on the table. She left the room, only to return a minute later with an omelette on a plate and a side dish of buttered potatoes.

'Spinach and onion. No pork,' she said as she set the meal down on the table. A three-legged stool in the corner of the room was dragged over. She patted the seat to indicate where Monika should sit, saying 'Eat up.'

Frau Lange left the room and once again locked the door behind her. Monika went to the table. This time, she ate the food eagerly. The omelette was soft and oily and to her hungry mouth tasted good. After eating, feeling somewhat revived, she began to look around the room more closely.

She went to the windows. There were two of them, looking out onto the backs of several other brick buildings. One floor below was a courtyard with laundry drying on a line. She tried to open each window in turn but both of them were sealed shut. She checked the drawers of the big chest with the vase on top. They opened with a dry scrape and were entirely empty but for a sprinkling of dust. She looked beneath the bed – there was nothing here but an old brass bed pan. She checked the bedclothes and found a nightgown neatly folded, along with a hand towel tucked under the covers.

She waited for an hour, expecting someone to come and instruct her on what would happen next, but no one came. She tried knocking on the door again, only half-heartedly this time. There was only silence from the corridor outside. She climbed into bed. There was nothing to do. The light outside was darkening, so she pulled the window curtains closed. After a while, she drifted off to sleep, waking and turning over in the folds of her bedclothes, fitfully sleeping through the night with the odd strange dream tucked in.

Sometime after dawn, an hour or so perhaps, Frau Lange came in carrying the same tablecloth as before. Instead of laying the table herself, the old woman left the tablecloth on the edge of the table and said, 'You can do it this time.'

Monika got out of bed and did what she was told. Now it was morning, she was relieved that the night's stay was over. She was going home today and expected to be leaving soon.

Frau Lange brought a breakfast of onion quiche with buttered bread on the side. There was also a small saucer of honey with a tiny silver spoon in it.

'Thank you,' Monika said as she sat at the table to eat.

'How was your sleep?'

'Broken.'

'Tonight will be better.'

Monika smiled. She thought of her bed at home, and her candles, writing desk and books. Tonight would be better, that was true. 'When will they take me home?' she asked.

'When you are ready.'

'I'm ready now.'

'What I mean to say is, when *they* are ready.'

'How long will that be? And where are my possessions? I should have them before I go back.'

'Trust me when I say this,' Frau Lange said, coming closer, her voice changing by a pitch. 'Nothing that might happen to you is a result of anything that you have done.'

Monika looked up. 'What do you mean by that?'

Frau Lange sighed, as if she'd been burdened with an impossible question.

'Frau Lange?'

'Will I get my things back today?' She thought about her parents and the suspicions that might be stirred if she came back without her belongings.

'Frankly,' Frau Lange said, 'I don't know anything about your things. What I do know is that you are going to stay here longer than you think. Tonight. Tomorrow night. Who knows for how long?'

'There must be a misunderstanding. The agreement was for one night.' Monika looked at the unshakable demeanour in Frau Lange's face and realised it was fruitless to argue. 'Where am I?' she asked.

'In Berlin.'

'Where am I exactly?'

Frau Lange refrained from answering.

'Can you let me go? I don't need to be taken home. I can find my own way without an escort.'

'I can't do that.'

'Why not? Please.'

'I am not in charge.'

Monika looked over to the open door with the key in the lock. There was nothing stopping her from dashing through that door right now. Frau Lange couldn't hope to catch her.

'Come with me,' Frau Lange said, noticing the direction of Monika's gaze. 'I can see that you want to know what's on the other side of that door.'

'Yes.'

The old woman gestured for Monika to follow. She led her along a corridor with doors on either side. The floor was wooden and dark and had a narrow rug running the entire length. They went past a small kitchen, inside of which Monika saw a stack of white plates, a large frying pan and an enormous tray of eggs.

'How many people are staying here?'

Frau Lange replied, 'Not many. They come and go every day.'

The end of the corridor opened onto a flight of stairs that went down and doubled back on itself. Soon enough they were stood in a hallway with ceramic tiles on the floor and a large wooden door with frosted glass panels on either side. It was the same hallway Monika had come through yesterday. On the other side of the door came the stifled sounds of the street outside.

Frau Lange pointed to the door and said, 'The only way out is through there. You'll have to wait for someone to open it from the other side.'

Monika went to the door and levered the handle. It was firmly shut and didn't move.

'How do you get out?' she asked.

'I don't. I live inside this building.'

'You never go out?'

'I go to the market every other day at ten in the

morning. If I'm not waiting at this door by that time, then I miss the chance.'

'It's like a prison here!'

'I've made a life here,' Frau Lange said, growing annoyed.

Monika then realised that the old woman before her had succumbed to the strange conditions of the building. Even if they were bound by the same rules, she could only hold onto the fact that her own circumstances were different. But how the outcome would materialise exactly, she was yet to discover.

15

The following day, Frau Lange shuffled into Monika's room and said, 'I've decided, it may help you to settle in better if we had dinner outside today.'

'I thought it was prohibited for me to leave this room?'

'It's a warm evening. We can go up to the roof.'

Together they went into the corridor where Frau Lange unlocked a small door, behind which a staircase ran upwards. It was dirty in the narrow staircase, with flies skipping over the surface of the walls and a terrible damp smell. The steps led to the flat-top roof of the building. There was nothing up there apart from a row of air vents and an empty gull's nest built up in one corner, but it was good to be outside. Monika could see the street down below. It was quiet, nearly empty, and quite desolate. She had no idea where in the city she was.

Frau Lange lifted a foldaway table from behind one of the air vents and deftly flipped it into a standing position. Then she disappeared down the staircase again.

Monika went to the roof's edge and looked down. She saw a truck parked opposite on the roadside, and further along the street a horse and cart shuffling into the distance. Suddenly, she was alert to the idea of escaping. Jumping was impossible as they were three floors up, but climbing down could be feasible and would undoubtedly test the strength in her legs and arms. If she was going to attempt anything she would have to act quickly.

She scouted the edge, left and right. Below, there was the ledge of a window frame she could balance herself on, if she could lower herself down. Maybe she could reach over to the pipes and scramble to the ground? It was difficult to say without trying.

A moment later, before Monika had finished the thought, Frau Lange returned. Monika pulled away from the roof's edge and pretended to smile. Frau Lange carried the white tablecloth and insisted that Monika should be the one to spread it over the table. She slowly unfolded it, all the time wondering if it was indeed possible to climb from the roof down to the street. All she needed was for the old woman to disappear again, it wouldn't take more than a few seconds.

The tablecloth fell around the edges of the table. To assist, Frau Lange took the corner of the cloth between her thumb and first finger and pulled it towards her with a slow jerk, then flattened it out again with her palm. 'You look unwell,' she said, looking up at Monika. 'Make sure you sleep tonight.' Then, coming up close and putting the back of her arthritic knuckles to Monika's cheek, 'We only live once in this world,' she said, with what Monika recognised as a touch of caring.

They ate their meal together in the open air with the trickle of street noise below. Midway through, Monika knocked her glass off the side of the table, hoping it would act as a decoy for Frau Lange to disappear again. But the old woman didn't budge and looked on unimpressed.

'Is this how you repay my kindness to you?'

'I must get out of here.' Monika looked directly into Frau Lange's misty eyes. 'I don't understand why I'm still here.'

'It is your boyfriend, is it not? The one they have taken you from?'

'Yes. Do you know about him?'

'We're not told very much.'

'They say he's a political radical and that he hates Jewish people.'

'How is that possible?'

'I don't know but I saw a photograph. None of it makes sense.'

Frau Lange placed her hand on top of Monika's and said, 'I'm sorry, but I don't know any more than you do.'

'What about Hannah Baumer? I want to speak to her.'

Frau Lange shook her head blankly. 'I don't know anyone called Hannah Baumer.'

'You must do,' Monika replied. 'The woman in the cream coat who had me sent here for protection. She works for the police. She will help me.'

'I'm sorry, I've never heard of her.'

'Then what about you? Can you help me get away?'

'Me?'

'I have to get out. Help me, please. Let me go.'

'I can't do that.'

'You must. I can climb over the edge right now. Just let me go. You could say that I tricked you and locked you in my room when you weren't looking. Come, we can put you in there right now.'

'No, no they will get rid of me if I do that. I will not be safe.'

'Surely the police won't harm you?'

'The police? It's not the police I work for.'

'Then who are they?'

'This place, these rooms, they belong to the *Braunhemden*.'

'The Brownshirts?' Monika said leaning forward.

'Yes, the *Sturmabteilung*. That's their official name.'

Monika was crestfallen. She knew they were the Nazi paramilitary. 'This is awful,' she uttered as she thought Arno might be part of the same mob.

'My late husband was a member of the Party,' Frau Lange explained. 'When he died, I came to work here. They give me a pension and I don't pay any rent. This is a good life for me. Running these rooms, is what keeps me in food and shelter. They are decent to me.'

'I thought I came here with the Prussian Police.'

'I don't know how you got here. Sometimes they hold meetings and I make them their food. They have a few offices on the first floor and the bedrooms of course. This is also a storage facility – they keep things like cigarettes here and other goods to be sold. It's their way of making some income for the Party.'

Monika listened as her shock and confusion rose.

Frau Lange stood up and walked to the edge of the rooftop. The sun had set and the evening air was beginning to cool. She coughed a couple of times, then took a breath deep into her lungs. 'It's not my place to break the rules,' she said, making her voice carry as if she was confirming something she'd been reflecting on for a long time. Then, looking back at Monika, she said, 'I respect the few privileges I've been given. They give me stability and I value that. But my dear girl, if I thought you were in danger, I would tell you.'

Upon hearing this, Monika's mind drifted to the two police officers from the hotel who had put her into the car back to Berlin. The woman, Hannah Baumer, seemed genuinely trustworthy. The man, on the other hand, that sorry ogre, had been most insistent about Arno's activities. If there was one person she didn't trust, it was him. He must be the link to the Nazis.

Frau Lange could see Monika was pensive. 'Perhaps you'd like to see where I live?' the old woman said, somewhat unexpectedly. 'You might find it more useful than you'd expect.'

16

Frau Lange led Monika through the building that seemed so empty and void of people it made the place feel ghostly. They reached a small annexe room two floors below and passed through a curtain of beads. It was like entering a different world. The room was filled from top to bottom with the strangest articles Monika had ever seen. It was nothing short of a treasure trove, a whole gamut of strange trinkets and worldly ornaments that hung on the walls and covered every square inch of flat surface.

Frau Lange went ahead and lit several oil lamps. Layers of semi-transparent drapes hung through the room, casting rays of light between them that cut the room into distinct parts depending on where the flickering light fell. In every corner, there were so many ornaments and odd objects that Monika didn't know where to step. It was as if the room was already too full to permit anything else to enter.

Frau Lange had no such problem as she moved among the clutter and planted herself in the centre of the room, pulling a sort of pirouette as she turned. It was the first time Monika had seen her express herself in any truly personal way, and she knew then that this room was Frau Lange's entire life.

Monika found the room intriguing. It was dark and

gothic, the opposite of modern things – beauty in utility, the Bauhaus philosophy of form arising out of function.

It was a fascinating place. On the walls were drawings, some of ancient figures – Plato, Ptolemy and Leonardo da Vinci. Next to them was a framed engraving of the Four Winds, with winged cherubs straining to expel breath from their inflated cheeks. Other wall hangings included zodiac charts and astronomical diagrams.

The objects on permanent display were not the end of it. Inside drawers were collections of amulets and talismans, some carved in wood, others made out of semi-precious stones such as sapphire, sardonyx and amethyst. Frau Lange took one of these amulets, with a small pendant of yellow-reddish amber, and hung it around Monika's neck by an old boot lace, telling her it would protect her heart and lungs against disease.

'What's that?' Monika asked, pointing to a metal pole that was bent into a right-angle and tapered at one end to a narrow flat-edged point. Frau Lange seemed especially pleased that Monika had picked out this object.

'That is one-half of a pair of dowsing rods. We use them to locate the energy lines of water. Now, where's the other one?'

Monika picked up the object. Her intuition told her it could be handy – not for finding underground rivers but for more immediate advantages. She noticed the point of the rod had the chiselled look of a screwdriver. With Frau Lange bent over looking for the other dousing rod, Monika slipped the one she was holding under her blouse.

'It's somewhere here and is bound to turn up,' Frau Lange said, straightening herself up. 'Did you take it?'

'Excuse me?'

'The rod?' Frau Lange pointed to the straight-edged

sag in Monika's top.

'I'm sorry,' Monika said feeling embarrassed. She began to pull the rod from out of her blouse.

'Sorry about what?' Frau Lange asked, patting the air with her hand, indicating that Monika should leave the metal rod where it was.

All of a sudden, the sound of footsteps marching came from the passage outside. Frau Lange blew out one of the oil lamps and gestured to Monika to hide behind one of the drapes. Monika crouched down and disappeared behind a screen, just as a Brownshirt entered the room.

'There you are Frau Lange. They want coffee upstairs straight away,' the man stated bluntly.

'Yes sir,' the old woman replied bowing her head.

The Brownshirt looked around the room. 'What a hovel this place is,' he said picking up an object with a look of disgust. He then threw it at Frau Lange, who remained still and submissive.

Monika scowled to herself, gripping the rod in her blouse.

'I'll be there presently, *Gefreiter*.'

At this the Brownshirt smirked and strode off out of her room into the cold corridor.

'It was a risk bringing you here.'

'I don't want to get you into trouble,' Monika said, handing the rod back.

'I've seen nothing. What I don't know about, I can't be blamed for,' Frau Lange replied. 'Come let's leave quickly.'

A short time later, Monika was back in her own room. Out of a growing sense of respect for Frau Lange, she waited for the old lady's footsteps to retreat from behind the locked door before she attempted anything. When all was completely quiet, she withdrew the dowsing rod from her clothes and immediately began to put it to use on the locked door.

She pushed the rod under the lock. Using the flat edge as a lever, the ceramic outer casing was easily prised away and loosened from the handle. She was pleased with its effect. The tool was working. Now to the intricacies of the actual mechanism. It was not easy. The metal rod was hardly made for twisting a rusted screw and simply turning it was near to impossible. But with persistence she found it was narrow enough to slot into the screw heads, and as she asserted more force the screw began to turn.

Sooner or later the inner metal plates were in pieces on the floor. But the task was far from complete. The door was still locked, the bolt still in place. She peered inside the shadowy crevice she'd managed to cleave open and tried to picture how the mechanism operated. Now she took the dowsing rod and began probing the inside of the lock. The bolt was old and loose in its casing; when she inserted the rod she was able to prise the end into a narrow gap and begin to scrape the bolt from left to right. It moved by tiny degrees, as drops of perspiration slipped down the temple of her forehead. She paused every so often, thinking she could hear someone approaching in the distance outside. Shifting on her knees, she folded her legs beneath her to regain her balance. The floor was cold but she pushed on until finally, the locked door was open.

17

Monika inched her way out. She kept her back close to the wall as she crept along the length of the corridor, whilst constantly checking over each shoulder. She had no idea if the building that held her was teeming with dangers or if it was, at this time, empty as the silence suggested.

She stopped outside one of the many doors. There was a reason she chose this particular door: on it was attached a hand-written notice that read *'Lieferungen'* – Deliveries. The key was still in the lock, so she turned it and the door opened. Inside was a narrow storeroom filled from floor to ceiling with boxes of cigarettes. The packaging on the cigarette boxes said *Sturm, Trommler Gold*.

She took one of the boxes which was about a foot long and turned it over in her hands. It must have contained about twenty small packets inside. To come upon this stock cupboard felt like a small breakthrough.

She hunted around the room, looking for something that might give her a clue as to what she could do next. Making a quick calculation, she estimated there were at least four-hundred boxes inside the room. As this was a storeroom, then sooner or later the cigarettes would be moved from here and transported elsewhere for distribution.

To conceal herself, she closed the door silently behind her. She pulled on a cord to switch on the electric light so she could explore more thoroughly. As she moved between the boxes, she eventually came upon a sheet of paper. This was what she was looking for: it was a distribution schedule, detailing collection and delivery points all over Berlin.

To anybody else this might have been an anonymous bureaucratic document, but to Monika it represented a passport to her escape. As she scanned the paper, she felt the strength of her resolve rising to the surface. Judging from the times and dates listed, the collection and delivery of cigarettes occurred twice a week, meaning the next delivery was in two days time. The paper showed a list of locations around the city written in abbreviations, which she took as a series of outlets that stocked the Nazis' brand. Her eyes moved over the list of establishments trying to decipher the names. As far as she could tell, her own district of Schöneberg, where her parents' house was located, was not listed.

Then she spotted an abbreviation she could finally make sense of: *F.B.Tmpl.* This must be Berlin-Tempelhof Airport. Her gaze became fixed on it like a kestrel hovering over a hunting ground. It was the only name she could be truly certain of. She'd been to the airport once with her father on a day-trip. They went to watch the great silver-winged birds come and go, one after another, at the world's busiest airport. That memory was happy and made her next decision an easy one. The choice was simple. From this point on, the airport was her goal.

She spent the next few minutes memorising the schedule as best as she could, re-visiting the list to make sure she hadn't missed anything else of significance. Next, she checked the shelving, stretching on her tiptoes and bending down with folded knees, searching for anything else that might be forged into another opportunity. It was without a doubt the best chance she had of making an escape, and as she understood this, an increased determination begin to unfold inside of her.

Her thoughts went like this: the cigarette storeroom would be accessed in two days time, probably first thing in the morning, maybe between seven and eight o'clock, since the first drop-off was listed as 8:30 in the morning. The movement of cigarettes meant the building doors would be open, its entrance hall traversed by outside visitors and its quiet corridors momentarily disturbed. Somewhere within this activity, she had to make her move.

The next day passed as the previous one had, an uncharted slide into morning, noon and night, with the industrialised street outside gradually falling into complete retirement. When the next dawn came, she took the rising sun as her cue. She dressed and began her preparations. After having restored the lock on the door two nights before, she returned to the arduous task of dismantling it again. An hour later, she was standing in the corridor. She brought the metal rod with her and tucked it behind her in the waistband of her skirt.

She closed the door to her room, turned the key to best disguise her absence and then made her way down the staircase to the front door that led to the hallway. As she had noted from seeing the entrance hall before, a small triangular nook in the corner – a sort of miniature cloakroom – would be a perfect place to conceal herself. She squeezed into the darkened space, wedging herself as deep inside as she could.

Then she waited. Without access to a clock, it was impossible to say how long she would have to stand there pressed into the shadows of the nook, but she kept her eyes peeled for an opportune moment to sneak out. She had come this far. A fierce pride as resolute as stone hardened within her. And at the same time, even if she'd worked out the schedule, she knew the circumstances were still unpredictable.

After around forty-five minutes, barely daring to breathe, she heard the sound of voices outside. The main door to the building opened and two men came in. They passed by Monika's hiding place and went straight for the staircase leading to the first floor. Monika emerged cautiously yet without hesitation. The front door was left open. She went through it quickly, out into the street where a black truck was parked on the roadside.

It was at this moment that the first hint of uncertainty made her think twice. Her intention was to smuggle herself to Tempelhof Airport inside the Nazi vehicle. From there she could make a telephone call, contact the police and finally go home to her parents. But now stood out in the street beside the unmanned truck, she wondered if it made more sense simply to run.

She looked up and down the road. She could go in either direction. She could be away from the building in seconds. Yet it was impossible to know which direction Berlin centre was. There were no signs and no road names. From the morning sun, she worked out the four points of the compass. If only she could see where the heart of the city was? Then she noticed a tram-line in the distance running in a curved arc across the ground. She thought she could follow the metal tracks and reach the next tram stop. There would be a sign, maybe even a map. But then again, it could be too far, meaning she would be more at risk of being picked up by the people she was escaping from.

If she ran, would they recognise her? How soon

would it be until they knew she was missing? It wouldn't be too long before Frau Lange would notice her missing when she brought in her breakfast. The old lady might delay telling them to increase her chances of escape.

Even so, Monika was aware her hesitation was costing her valuable time. She knew it was best to stay out of sight. She made up her mind, gently prising open the rear hatch of the truck. It was now or never, and on that thought she climbed inside to find somewhere to hide.

18

Monika crawled down onto her knees and hunched down beneath one of the wooden benches where a canvas sheet was half-folded and crushed into the corner. She used the sheet to cover herself up as best as she could, feeling its rough surface, which was mottled with mould spots. The floor of the truck was peppered with spilt sawdust and flakes of cigarette tobacco.

Within minutes she heard the sound of boxes being loaded around her. She squeezed under the sheet as keenly as she could, then remained motionless. She resisted looking out from her concealment, but she could hear the continuing rumble of activity and the rocking of the truck as the men climbed in and out. Eventually, the loading of cargo seemed to come to an end, and after some time of stacking and sorting, the engine started up. Monika cast her mind back to the delivery drop-off list and worked out how many stops she would have to wait before they arrived at the airport.

After about half an hour they reached the first drop-off point. The truck hatch door opened, and then she could hear the muffled hum of voices and the sound of crate boxes being lifted off. The hatch was closed again and the truck resumed its journey. The vehicle swayed and roared along.

Lying in the shadows made by a tiny window in the

truck, Monika took the canvas sheet from her face and came up for some air. Glancing around she could see the name *Sturm Zigaretten* printed across the piled up crates with the SA logo stamped beneath. The company had been founded by the Nazi Party and as Frau Lange had said, was a way of funding the Party's political activities. And there was Monika right in the middle of its operation. She was now a stowaway, travelling with the enemy before she could finally flee once they reached the airport.

She cloaked herself again as the vehicle reached another stop. The shutter door on the truck was then lifted up by the two men as she listened to the rough chatter. Suddenly unable to hold her breath, she sneezed from the back of the truck, causing her to shrink into a ball. Everything then fell quiet, after which there was suddenly the sound of shouts and boxes being smashed.

Monika could hear the names of the cigarette brands she'd seen in the storeroom – *Trommler*, *Alarm*, *Sturm* and *Neue Front* – being cried out in what seemed like fits of rage. Unable to ignore the commotion, Monika found a narrow tear in the canvas and glimpsed through. From what she could see the two delivery men kept passing in and out of a shop carrying wooden boxes and throwing them onto the pavement. Then they started breaking the shop windows before muscling into the back of the truck to unload the new stock. The punishment was for selling rival brands, a mistake that the threatened shopkeeper would never repeat.

Monika dug her thumbnails into her palms to stop the flood of dread she was feeling. She couldn't wait to get to the airport now. Then after two more stops, she began to make out the distinct whir of an aeroplane propeller passing overhead. The sound grew louder. She pictured one of the flying machines sweeping down out of the clouds and landing its rubbery tyres on the airport runway. To hear them was a relief and felt like the promise of liberation opening up around her. All that remained was the question of when.

The truck drove on, turning corners, slowing down and speeding up again. At last, it came to a halt and the door was lowered. She allowed herself to peel back the sheet a little in order to see more of what was going on. It was still dark behind the boxes, but if she craned her neck she could make out a triangle of sky between the wall of boxes and the roof of the truck. Through this patch of sky, she saw the broad white wings of an aeroplane coming into land.

This had to be it. This was the moment. They were on the airfield now, or as close to it as she could be. She pushed the canvas sheet off her head and slid from beneath the bench.

More of the cigarette boxes were being offloaded. Only two stacks stood between her and the outside world. For a split second, she was tempted to make a dash for it and clamber over the boxes in a frantic rush. But no, she would wait and try to leave discreetly without being seen or heard.

She crouched on her knees with the grimy sheet still drawn up around her shoulders. The two delivery men were now stood along the side of the truck; she could hear them talking and the noise of striking matches as they lit up. She began to edge around the side of the remaining boxes, and as quietly as she could, manoeuvred along the bench towards the exit. She could see the full aperture of the opening now, and through it, the horizontal stretch of runway between the large swathes of grass and sky. There were three aeroplanes winding up in the far distance, and beyond them the low stretch of airport buildings.

She carefully lowered herself down to the ground. The delivery men were still smoking and oblivious to her presence. She made her way along the opposite side of the truck, constantly checking around, keeping her body pressed close to the metal flank that shielded her until she was as far removed from the men as possible.

Then suddenly around the truck corner the face of one of the delivery men appeared directly in front of her. Monika froze whilst the man was shocked and angry-looking. 'What are you doing here?' he said in a tone that trailed into bemusement. His face was long and his jaw was misaligned.

Monika didn't reply. She took hold of the metal rod still slotted against her back and using the end that was flattened to a wedge, thrust it directly into the man's upper arm. His thick jacket cushioned most of the impact, but there was enough force to penetrate his flesh by a quarter of an inch, causing him to yell out and clutch himself in pain.

Then she ran with all her might into the open space of the airfield. She ran across the grass with the coiled energy of a spring not yet released. A mist of cool rain started to fall. She ran as fast as she could. A fierce, straight-lined dash, unrelenting, undaunted. It was only as she felt she'd achieved her escape that she turned to see the other delivery man pursuing her, bearing down on her twice as fast as she could run.

Nothing looms so terribly as a stranger chasing after you. As she ran she could picture him closing in on her with his heavy boots thumping on the soft green turf. She waited to feel his arm hook around her, to be scooped up, lifted back and returned to her captivity in cruel, violent retribution.

But giving up was not allowed. She kept running and didn't look behind because to do so could affect her pace by a fraction. She just needed to cross this stretch of grass and reach the grey-box building – an aeroplane hanger presumably – where she could see a car and several people frozen in the distance – her saviours, whoever they were.

An incoming propeller plane gurgled overhead, descending through the wind above her. It swooped in a great arc as the engine noise squeezed and elongated, dropping a pitch as it sped over. She ducked her head instinctively and raced on. Her feet bounced across the grass, and as the sound from the aeroplane diminished, she had the sense that she had gained some distance from her pursuer.

She turned to look around and found the man to be fifty yards behind, bent over with his hands on his knees gasping for breath. He'd given up. Her heart was racing as she slowed down. Then, at the same moment, she looked up ahead and saw the glistening shape of a car travelling across the turf towards her. As it drew closer, it pulled up a short distance away and from its rear door a woman stepped out. Monika knew her immediately. That immaculate face and cream raincoat she trusted. Hannah Baumer.

She went towards the car with relief settling in her chest like a wave cresting. She ran with ease, as if the wind was pushing her, as the end of her journey lay right ahead. Monika had made her escape and now the police had come to return her home.

19

Within moments, Monika had left the breezy airport surroundings and was sat on the leather seat of the car alongside Hannah Baumer, whose scent of cologne had all the sweet warmth of a summer garden.

'How did you know I was here?' Monika asked after a few moments, knowing it had to be more than a coincidence that the police had appeared. She noticed the car was driving slowly back to the airport terminal. She wanted to turn and check that the coast was now clear.

'You don't need to worry, we're here now,' the woman said. 'That was very close.'

Monika restored her composure as the tension within her began to slip away from her. She'd been awake for several hours and her throat suddenly felt bone-dry. All she could think of was returning to her family home and being back in the calm surety of her parents' affection. It didn't matter how she was going to explain herself to them. Dealing with their consternation over her trip with Arno was nothing compared to the ordeal she'd just gone through. They would understand that when she explained it all.

'What happened?' she asked Baumer all of a sudden. 'I don't understand. Fours days ago, I thought I was going home.'

'I have some explaining to do,' Baumer replied. Her voice sounded apologetic, which is what Monika expected. Something went wrong along the line. The blame probably lay with the sack-of-potatoes policeman. She expected Baumer to feel contrition. That made sense.

'I'm sorry you had to go through all of that,' Baumer said, as if she could read Monika's thoughts. 'We were supposed to protect you but you were betrayed. That was my fault.'

'Was it him? Was it your colleague that handed me over to the Nazis?'

'Don't worry about that for now.'

'I feel filthy from that truck,' Monika said. She had some right to complain. Her parents – when they found out – would certainly want to take the whole matter further.

She gazed out of the window and gave a little shake of her head. What an experience! But it was over now. Her bravery and intelligence had delivered her from her detention. She was free.

As the car drove through Berlin, she began to imagine how this event might mark the start of a new phase for her family. Once the appropriate complaint against the authorities had been made, her father would probably recruit the expertise of his legal friends and other sharp-toothed plaintiffs – after which she could foresee the beginnings of their Berlin life coming to an end.

Perhaps it was inevitable. The last few years had been a difficult and uncertain time. It was common knowledge among her community that the Jewish population was despised by some quarters of the wider city. What was unknown was the question of exactly how it would materialise in her own life. For she didn't feel overtly oppressed by the situation, whatever it was that was emerging, in fact in some ways she'd moved against it. Jew-haters seemed to have other targets in mind other than young women like herself. Or was it simply that she'd grown used to the incessant prejudice and refused to let it dominate her?

She remembered a bus journey from a few months earlier, when one of the other passengers, who couldn't have been much older than she was – just a young man on the other side of the aisle – began talking about the 'corruption of German blood.' He was speaking to his friend sat beside him. The friend said that Jews made up only one per cent of the population, which meant that the 'Jewish question' was not so important as some made it out to be. At this, the man replied 'Yes, but they are prone to interfering in our culture. Something about the German race makes us particularly susceptible, perhaps because we are too trusting. We're not like the Latin races; they defend themselves more vigorously. For Germans, the Jews are a corrupting force precisely because we are innocent. That cannot be tolerated.'

Talk like this sometimes made Monika feel that the easiest thing was to deny who she was. Even if it could be taken as a shameful act – one that her parents would refuse to endorse – to her it seemed like the most expedient path, one which would keep her inner self intact. She knew herself and was proud of her roots deep down.

Even so, after this event, she began to wonder if their time in Berlin would come to an end. They had relatives in other countries: her mother had siblings in Sweden and a cousin in Belgium. Her father's brother was planning to move to America. She could imagine foreign towns being mentioned, places she'd heard of but never visited. 'It's clear that we are not welcome in our own country anymore,' she could hear her father saying at the dinner table. 'Just look what happened to Monika. Taken by the Nazis! Do you think it was coincidence how they treated her? Leaving her a prisoner in some safe-house that was nothing but a den for – who knows what?'

These conversations were imminent. If there was one thing her parents liked to do, it was to rake over everything to get to the bottom of things, especially when it came to the rights and treatment of their people. Monika felt exhausted by the thought.

For now, sat inside the motor car with Hannah Baumer, it was enough to slip into the tidal wave of relief. The car travelled through the city suburbs, trundling over tram tracks and pausing at road junctions. She felt the comfort of feeling safe.

After half an hour, the car took a turning down a residential avenue, through some countryside and then up a stone rubbled road. It slowed down to a stop and the engine shut off. Monika could hear another vehicle closing in behind them. She turned around and looked through the rear window, and to her horror saw the cigarette delivery truck parking up behind them. She rolled down the window and saw the same building she had escaped from only two hours before. She recoiled as she looked in disbelief at the woman beside her.

Baumer said nothing and gave only a cruel calculating smile.

'What's going on?' Monika asked contentiously.

'We'll have to watch you more closely from now on,' Baumer replied.

'Who are you? Whose side are you on?'

'I'm on my own side,' Baumer said bluntly, as she pulled out a compact mirror from her purse and checked herself over.

The two delivery drivers came to the car door, opened it and urged Monika out onto the street. One of the men was still clutching his arm from the injury she'd given him. Baumer told them not to hurt her.

They took her into the building and pulled her up the staircase that she recognised all too well. She tried to resist, yelling and pleading, but their force was relentless. This time they put her into a smaller, darker room, and when the door was shut, she could hear a metal bar being bolted across the front of it. She was back where she started. Confined and alone.

20

The interior of Monika's new room was badly lit. The window was sealed shut and so murky with dust and soot that at first it was hard to know if it was day or night. A single electric light bulb hung from the ceiling with no shade around it. There was nothing in the room but for a bed with a torn pillow on it. She had never felt so desperate in all her life.

She had been moved to a different part of the warehouse building. Every so often, voices came and went outside the door, then there were new voices with new business at hand, brief echoes of something official being said.

A day passed. Possibly a second. Frau Lange no longer visited. Instead, Monika's meals were brought in by a boyish-looking soldier who was almost certainly younger and more naive than she was. Most of the time he wore a cowed expression, as if he expected to be startled at any moment and was constantly waiting for her to object to his presence. But he was courteous and patient. He always knocked and never knocked more than once, never hurried her to come to the door, just waited outside with her tray of food.

She felt grateful for the soldier's civility. He wouldn't tell her his name or anything else about himself. His face was unblemished like a youth in bloom. It was clear he was acutely obedient to whatever orders he'd had handed down to him. And he never once showed any type of emotion.

Yet she waited for these rare moments of contact. The new room they'd put her in was so improbably sparse and unpleasant it seemed to deny her even the possibility of optimism. She wished she had something from the outside world, something to remind her that her life beyond these walls was still waiting for her. In these circumstances, she found it hard to form thoughts of hope, let alone plan what she could do next. At least the young soldier gave her some respite from this absorption into nothingness.

Each day he came, bringing her breakfast, lunch and dinner, which were barely meals at all and were usually cold by the time she ate them. She tried to make conversation with him, but the boy was far too duty-bound to break out of his muteness.

It was hard to say what was happening to her. Her clever mind refused to offer any answers. It was like her whole being was blunted. The only thing she could dwell on was whether she was one step closer to her reckoning or if, with every hour, she should be grateful that she remained unharmed and still alive. Was it over or was it still to come, her fate, whatever it was supposed to be?

She found the weight of the uncertainty to be far heavier at night, when the electric bulb was switched off remotely, making the room feel so dark and distant it was like being in a prison cell in the middle of nowhere. The light went off at around ten o'clock, at which the four walls of the room closed in tightly around her. It wasn't black but a swarming, impenetrable ink of darkest blue. She couldn't see her hand, even when she held it right in front of her face.

Sleeping in these conditions was impossible. Most of

all, she feared someone entering the darkness. It took an age for the morning to come; when at last the dawn light began to show at the clogged-up window, she still questioned it. It was only when she could hear the rattle and footsteps of morning routines that she allowed herself to feel a reprieve that another night was over. It was like coming up for air after being submerged underwater.

Sometimes, she could remember what it was like to be free. These were the only thoughts that came with any clarity. She remembered moving through the hustle and bustle of Berlin's streets. And she remembered the holidays with her parents, hiking along mountain valleys and finding shade beneath a row of pine trees, leaning over a map alongside her father, wondering where their freedom would take them next. Were these memories or dreams? Did she summon them or were they summoning her? It didn't really matter.

One morning, when the soldier came with breakfast, she noticed what looked like spots of blood over the left shoulder of his uniform. He refused to look her in the face, but it was clear that something out of the ordinary had happened to him.

Whispering, she asked him what it was. He said nothing back, only gave an expression of deliberate vagueness. His pride had been hurt, that was obvious. She cautiously examined the flecks of blood, which formed a line like an archipelago of islands across a map. Then she saw that his nose had been recently cleaned up and he had bruising beneath his eye too.

'Did someone hit you?' she asked. Such a direct question would go one of two ways. He'd either turn angry or relent.

'The Oberführer hit me with his pistol,' the SA boy

admitted. It was the first time he'd said anything about himself.

'Why?'

'I don't know.'

'Does it hurt?'

'Not really. I just have an ache in my head.'

'What's his name, your General?'

'Hessen. I don't like him. He's a monster.'

'Who is he?'

'He's in charge of the Berlin SA.'

The boy wiped his sleeve under his nose and sniffed. Monika thought he was going to lash out in embarrassment, but with a deep intake of breath, he stood tall and composed himself. Just then, footsteps along the corridor alerted their attention to an oncoming figure.

'It's him,' the soldier murmured, as his face stiffened with fear.

'Go quickly,' Monika said.

The approaching figure called out something inaudible. Immediately, the young soldier marched in the opposite direction, once or twice breaking into a skip to quicken his step.

The man's footsteps drew closer. Monika stepped back and braced herself. Was this the moment she had been waiting for?

As he came into view, he introduced himself. 'I'm General Hessen. But you may call me Heinrich or Count. Whichever you prefer.'

Monika looked up. He was tall, smart, and had a small scar on the middle of his forehead.

Hessen presented his hand and with it gripped Monika's chin between his thumb and fingers. 'So you're my little prize, are you? I wonder how much you'll be worth to me in the end?'

Monika pushed the clasp of his fingers away from her chin.

'I'm not worth anything,' she objected. 'Not to you.'

'Come, come, where's your smile?' Hessen said, toying with her. 'There must be one in there somewhere. Let me see if I can find it. I'm told you tried to escape? That tells me you have a home to go to and a doting family waiting for you. Not a bad thing at all. You want to be back with them as soon as you can, don't you? Well, don't worry my little Jew, you will. When the time is right. Just pray your family does the right thing by you.'

The Nazi gazed down on Monika, who glared back at him. His face was lean and he had sunken cheeks.

'I suppose,' Hessen went on in a tone of resignation, 'that being locked up in here is bound to make anyone miserable.'

'What am I doing here?' she asked.

'Raising your own price. The longer you stay, the more valuable you become.'

Monika was speechless. The man who stood in front of her had the coldest and most arrogant manner she had ever known. Did he mean to ransom her and threaten her family? For what? To fund his treacherous fascist campaign?

'Now, what if I told you could have whatever meal you like tonight? Your choice. Whatever your heart desires. What will it be?'

Monika refused to answer.

The General laughed. 'It's not a trick! I don't want you starving to death. That's not what I want at all!'

Monika shook her head.

'Don't be obstinate girl. Think of your family.'

'What do you know of my family?'

'I know they will pay the consequences if you don't

cooperate,' he said coming up close.

Monika understood his meaning and backed away from him.

'Now, we're having a party tonight. There's no reason why you should miss out. Now, doesn't that get a smile?'

Monika forced her lips to part and raised her cheeks.

'There. I told you there was one in there, didn't I? You could have *schweinshaxe*, *eisbein* or *senfbraten*?

His facetious suggestions made Monika look away. 'You know I can't eat any of those.'

'Oh, okay,' he said feeling amused. 'No pork!'

'I can't eat anything!'

'Suit yourself,' Hessen smirked. He left her, humming a tune to himself.

That night, as she lay there in the dark, she could hear the stifled sounds of the party in some distant part of the building. There was music and singing, clapping and cheering, a menagerie of sounds that lasted deep into the night. Then, at some untold hour, she was terrified to hear the metal bar on the door of her room being unbolted and the door open. Then in its frame she saw the silhouette of a strange man enter.

PART III – ARNO

21

'My name is Arno Hiller. I was born near the city of Mönchengladbach. My father was a factory clerk born into a German family. My mother had mixed Dutch and German parentage. My uncle on my mother's side was a successful art dealer in Hanover. My family moved to the outskirts of Berlin where I attended the local school until the age of seventeen. Whilst there, I specialised in the history of art.

In 1930, I attended my first meeting of the National Socialist German Workers' Party. I joined the Party in September of that same year, volunteering my time to disseminate leaflets and manage rallies.

Presently I live alone in Berlin, having recently worked for the engineering company Orenstein & Koppel as a factory worker, manufacturing railway vehicles. I am currently employed by my uncle as a clerk in the Berlin branch of his art dealership. I am twenty three years old.'

In his attic room, Arno read the single sheet of paper contained inside the dossier that had just been delivered to him. The words of the man who gave it to him rang in his ears. *'You will begin tomorrow.'*

His eyes rolled over the typed words on the page and he felt a sudden chill creep down the back of his neck. It seemed the Prussian Police knew his whole life story –

except they'd embellished it with details of their own making.

It was true that he was born in a village near Mönchengladbach and that his parents hailed from Germany and the Netherlands. He'd also worked at the Orenstein & Koppel factory for a short time. But he'd never joined the Nazi Party, not officially in any case. Nor did he study the history of art. The extract gave details of his life – and yet given a twist, as if describing an invisible twin who had lived a different life alongside his.

He switched the paper over to find there was something attached to the back – a ticket for a lecture taking place in a hall on Alexander Platz. On the face of the ticket was the title of the lecture: *Public Discourse on the Elixir of Life*. The start time was seven o'clock that evening. The hour had been twice underlined in green ink. He looked at his wristwatch and saw he had less than fifty minutes to get there. '*Don't be late*,' he'd been warned by the stranger.

He dressed and shaved. For supper, he ate two boiled eggs with a thick slice of vollkornbrot. He took the letter and ticket and folded them into his pocket, then dashed down the five flights of stairs, three steps at a time, into the cool air of the open street.

He made it to the lecture hall on Alexander Platz with only minutes to spare. He was intrigued to know why he had been sent to the dusty lecture hall to listen to some professor make a speech on the *Elixir of Life*.

The lobby was packed with eager-faced patrons pushing to get into the main hall. Arno noticed the man ahead of him had only one leg and was perched up on crutches. As the swarm of people shuffled forward, so the man lifted his crutches and swung himself a step onward.

Years ago, you'd see plenty of men like that, some hobbling on sticks and some in wheelchairs, some with an arm missing and some with no arms at all, their shirtsleeves pinned back at the shoulders. Arno especially noticed the men with eye-patches, since to him they seemed to carry an inexplicable nobility. And tonight it seemed odd there were so many ex-military men around with black triangles on their faces.

Finally, he reached the entrance and handed over his ticket to a man wearing a bright red tie. As Arno went inside, he glanced quickly at the poster pasted onto the wall: *The Secrets of Never-Ending Life*. 'What am I doing here?' he thought to himself.

The hall was long and wide. It had a high ceiling that was curved like a barrel and was lit by rows of white bulbs in half-moon crescent shapes. The hall was almost full. There were only a few vacant chairs dotted about, mostly in the middle of the rows. Along the outer aisles, more people stood, unable or unwilling to reach the last stranded chairs.

Arno checked where he was sitting – row S, seat 12 – before cutting along the row. People stood up and sat down again like dominoes to let him through. Then, settling in, he watched as the man in the red tie who had checked his ticket at the door walked all the way along the central aisle to the stage: he was in fact the speaker everyone had come to see.

The lecturer cleared his throat and the hubbub of the audience turned quiet. Now stood at a lectern, he prepared his papers before the eyes of the five-hundred spectators. He took a sip from a glass of iced water before delivering his opening lines, which he did with as much gravity as possible:

'My intention today is to disclose how anyone of us might live beyond the usual terrestrial span. Many have dreamed of never-ending life, but up until now, it has seemed like an impossible fantasy. Today, I intend to rid you of that disbelief.'

He was clearly proud of his latest theory, leaving great spaces between each word and holding onto syllables with protracted emphasis. As he spoke, he began to thumb through the stack of papers in front of him and spread them across the lectern.

The audience watched on in purest expectation. Most of all, it was the speaker's principle declaration, to know the secret of 'surviving to untold ages', that gave the whole room its sharp mood of anticipation.

'The very fact of death is utterly regretful. A force within us enables us to grow, and yet it is this very force that leads us into decline. Thus, strength gives way to weakness, and life gives way to death.'

Everywhere, heads nodded in agreement, the hush of sober recognition.

Beside him, Arno noticed an elderly gentleman who wore a wine coloured velvet jacket, squirming in his seat as a mood of expectancy swept through the room. The old man turned and gave an awkward pouting smile, as if to discharge a quantity of pent-up impatience.

The lecturer moved through his discourse by careful degrees, couching his argument in claim and counterclaim. The ideas grew more technical and came in a flow that became more complicated. Yet steadily the crux of the argument emerged, summed up in the following passage:

'Through my research, it has become apparent to me that as all human beings age, their sexual potency at first increases and then regresses. I have observed a profound correlation between the waning of sexual need and the onset of human ageing. If only we can revive the sexual libido then we may also stop the ageing process in its tracks. Our laboratory work, then, has been based upon reviving the sexual vivacity of individuals to awaken the elixir of life that lies deep within us all.

'My team and I have performed a series of experiments on laboratory rats and have successfully rejuvenated senile male rats through bilateral vasectomy. Within a few weeks of the operation, the previously lethargic, under-weight and almost lifeless rats were once again active. They had developed glossy new furs and gained additional weight. Importantly, their sexual interest was also renewed. And in case you are wondering, females are also applicable to this procedure. Despite the difference in reproductive systems, we have found that the same remarkable effects can be achieved by a destruction of the germinal cells of the ovary by low-dose radiation.'

So there it was. The crowd fell silent.

'We look forward to the renewal of the entire German people through this procedure,' the lecturer concluded with a flourish. 'We have overcome death!'

Members of the audience, who had listened ardently throughout, began stirring. There was a distinct air of unease in the room. Universal vasectomy and radiation treatment were not the secret to eternal life they were hoping for.

A short time later, with his discourse fully unravelled, the speaker invited questions from the floor. But it was obvious now that the audience's position had changed. They wanted *The Cup of Life*, not a scalpel blade to their sexual organs. The speaker stood uncomfortably at the podium, his hands moving back and forth along the rim of the lectern. Perhaps he was more used to an audience of doctors and academics, not this assorted crowd of wishful thinkers.

The old man next to Arno turned on his seat and

presented a churlish sort of grimace, indicating that he was sorely unimpressed with the argument.

Others in the audience murmured words of disgruntlement.

'What a waste of time,' one voice shouted.

'Rubbish!' another voice at the front called out.

Rows of the audience began to boo. A tide of ill-feeling was gaining momentum.

Now the lecturer turned to one of the event organisers. After a moment's discussion, he dismounted his small podium and hastily disappeared behind a curtain. The scheduled question and answer session was abandoned, and the audience, growing more animated, was left to make up its own mind.

Arno's neighbour gave his summing up without reserve. 'Frankly, I wished I hadn't come. How preposterous!' he said.

A middle-aged woman turned around and spoke, as if in response, 'I travelled all the way from Leipzig to listen to this charlatan.'

The old man sat next to Arno continued his vague exchange. 'I'm disappointed how much I have pinned my hopes on this lecture. Of course, that lecturer is in trouble now,' the old man said, addressing Arno directly. 'They won't like it.'

'Who won't?'

'The management. They don't like it when things go astray.'

'Actually, my ticket came from a friend of a friend,' Arno said, wheedling his way in. 'It didn't actually say who the organisers were.'

'The Party of course. The National Socialists. They're running the whole thing.'

Arno nodded.

'Oh yes. Most people here are members. Aren't you?'

Arno remembered the letter in his pocket. 'As a matter of fact, I am.'

At this point, there was activity at the front of the room. The stage was being rearranged and people began to grow excited.

Arno stretched himself on his chair. 'What's happening?'

'It's a big-wig from the Party. We are privileged today. Hermann Göring no less.'

Arno knew the name, of course. One of Hitler's men-of-action, a key player in the Munich Putsch, someone who'd risen through the ranks all the way towards the top.

'He was a war hero, wasn't he?' Arno said, sensing the atmosphere in the room change.

'One of the Luftstreitkräfte's best pilots. He once landed a baron onto a frozen lake in a snowstorm. A real dare devil. He won a seat in the Reichstag and sits as the Party leader in the lower house. He has the entire SA looking out for him.'

Arno looked around. He became aware of uniformed men scattered in pairs throughout the hall, all in the same khaki-brown, each with a red band on his arm emblazoned with the swastika symbol. In his rush, he hadn't noticed them before. Some of them held clubs; others had short batons pushed under their belts. They seemed keyed up, undoubtedly thanks to the presence of Göring.

'They're in awe of his military success,' the old man said. 'Some call them thugs but they're here for their leader. To make sure the whole event goes without a glitch. You'd better not be a Communist tonight. Or that poor lecturer, for that matter.'

Arno got to his feet as the activity in the hall grew, with many of the older soldiers cheering Göring's arrival.

He made his way to the front of the hall through the huddle of bodies to see what was happening. He immediately recognised Göring's face from photographs but had never seen him in person before. He was broad shouldered and carried more weight around his belly than his press photos let on. He had a wide face and a high forehead. And there was that unmistakable slithering smile, one that appeared in place at a moment's notice, seeming to pull the rest of his face towards it like a drawstring.

As the honoured guest of the occasion, Göring was presented with a gift, wrapped in brown paper. He tore back the paper and held up a painting encrusted in a gold frame, which he then clutched to his chest in an expression of zeal. The audience around him applauded and called enthusiastically for a speech. Arno continued to advance his way forward and noticed the old gent trailing behind, scrambling to keep pace.

Göring had by now succumbed to pleas for a few words and was speaking in noble airs about the importance of science for the future of the German people. He allowed himself a moment of political speculation too: 'The key to our climb to power will be the removing from office of the Communists and Catholics who currently reside there. I hope you will join me in this cleansing, which is long overdue.'

The crowd then applauded and clapped at his proposal. Arno cringed inside. He wanted to erase that smile off Göring's face. Overcome with hatred, he then felt a hand grab the top of his shoulder. He looked around and saw the face of the old gent. 'Allow me to pass will you.'

Arno leaned aside, letting the man push himself forward until he was climbing onto the stage. After another moment, he was stood beside Göring.

It was only then that Arno saw that the two men knew each other. He was astonished to see Göring turn and embrace the old man, and with rather overdone enthusiasm, kiss him on the forehead as if he was embracing his own child. From there, Göring took hold of the painting he'd just been presented and showed the image to the old man, who clearly admired the object, running his fingers discreetly over the painting and pointing out areas of interest within it.

Then the old man looked up and caught Arno's eye among the crowd. Perhaps it was the way the spotlight glinted but at that moment he was sure he saw the old gent give him a wink.

22

The audience dispersed into the Berlin night, under the neon lights of a nearby cabaret show. The words *Tanz Kabarett* glowed red and gold, shimmering in the glossy rain-soaked street.

Arno left the lecture hall feeling stirred. He was back in the midst of Nazi radicalism, and getting a first-hand glimpse of Göring gave him an indication of just what he was dealing with.

As he walked, he came across a late-night bakery and went inside. On display there was a great glass cabinet layered with cheesecakes and all types of stollen, magenbrot biscuits and marzipans. He picked out two franzbrötchen cakes with a sudden taste for some buttery pastry and cinnamon. He went to a bench and took big bites. But when he recognised the second cake he'd bought would ordinarily have been for Monika, he quickly lost his appetite.

It was nine o'clock in the evening and the city was lighting up all around him. He noticed two prostitutes across the road exchanging money with a man in an over-sized woollen cap. Arno guessed he was their drug dealer, as a little packet of white powder was passed from his pocket into the gloved hand of one of the women.

Just then, a man's voice addressed him from behind.

'Berlin can be a gruesome place at times,' the voice said colourfully. 'But the cakes are second to none!'

Arno turned to see the face of the old man from the lecture hall. He was slight and entirely bald but for a wispy rim of brown hair, which in the light of the streetlamps was obviously dyed. His eyes were pale and his nose was turning grey from the tip upwards.

'May I introduce myself?' the man said. 'My name is Lassner. Herr Mattias Lassner.'

'Pleased to meet you,' Arno replied.

Herr Lassner took the liberty of sitting down on the bench beside Arno. He crossed his thin legs as if he intended to stay for a while, and adjusted his neck scarf as he spoke. 'It never ceases to amaze me how brazen some of these folk are.' He glanced at the prostitutes over the road. 'I think they *want* to be noticed.'

Arno smiled at the man's words.

'It wouldn't surprise me if that stash over the road was smuggled in by a certain political party,' the old man said, with a crisp edge of excitement to his voice.

The mention of bootlegging instantly took Arno's thoughts to the question of Vendetta. Lassner was clearly on amicable terms with Göring. And Arno could only assume that anyone with such a close tie with Göring was a deeply-embedded member of the Party. Making a quick calculation of events, he sat back on the bench and looked Herr Lassner straight in the eyes, ready to take the opportunity to find out more.

'You never told me your name young man?'

'It's Hiller. Arno Hiller.'

'Then answer me this Herr Hiller: Did you understand the theory?'

Arno looked at the old man quizzically.

'Infinite life? The lecture! I have to admit, I couldn't take it seriously at all.'

'Oh, the lecture. Well, it was unexpected,' Arno said vaguely. 'Quite outlandish, even in this day and age.'

'Forever young? It may sound rosy but it's completely far-fetched. The older you get, the more you realise that part of living is making way for the young to come through. For me, life is much like a garden…' Lassner trailed off without finishing his sentence.

Arno wasn't listening. His thoughts were edging towards Monika and the question of Vendetta. What was this old Nazi's involvement? All he really wanted was to find out more about infiltrating the Party.

'Herr Lassner, I wonder if you'd take a drink with me? I'd be interested in your views, politically speaking.'

Lassner gave a wry, if slightly furtive smile. His set of false teeth came out of position, which he eased back into place with the knuckle of his thumb. 'I know just the place,' he said, tapping Arno's arm with his big white fingers.

Directly above their heads, a sudden clap of thunder sounded. Dark clouds brewed above the electric lights. At the same moment, it began to rain, spitting at first but quickly building into a deluge. They stood up from the bench and briskly moved towards a set of doors nearby.

'Come on in,' Lassner said, guiding Arno with his hand on his back and leading him through the revolving door. 'The cloakroom is this way. We can dry off in there,' he said. They passed through into a hotel lobby, when suddenly the old man's weary eyes were no longer ashen and he seemed to grow by an inch. Lassner took off his coat and scarf. In the same instant, a comb appeared and he was carefully arranging his damp hair into fine ridges over the round of his head. Immediately, he had taken on a different aspect. Arno saw a proud-looking gentleman, immaculately dressed, with a neat crown of brown hair that stood out in an elegant way against his pale, ageing skin.

'They will serve us coffee through here,' Lassner said, pointing ahead. He seemed to know the place well.

Arno was guided to a corner table in the lounge area and shown to a seat. The lounge was mainly empty, though a few others had arrived out of the rain along with them. A cigarette seller was doing the rounds, calling out '*Zigaren, zigaretten*' in a wavering voice. He came over, only for Lassner to wave him away. Lassner took a moment to arrange himself, unbuttoning his inside waist-jacket and leaning forward with his arms tipping over his knees.

'I was impressed to see you know Göring,' Arno began.

'It is a position of honour I hold,' Lassner replied proudly.

Arno widened his eyes as if trying to imply something significant that he hoped Lassner would elaborate on.

'We have known one another for many years,' Lassner explained. 'Old friends, you might say.'

Arno had a simple question that kept returning to him like the beating of a moth against a lamp. 'Do you also work for him? For the Party that is?'

'I support the German way.'

'And what way is that?' Arno pressed plainly.

'The way of justice in our country.'

'As do I,' Arno said, dissatisfied with the answer given to him.

Herr Lassner glanced about him and betrayed a hint of furtiveness. 'But I can't pretend that knowing Göring doesn't have its advantages.'

'Like what?'

'I suppose you'd say the favour of having a reputation, which goes a long way in my line of business.'

'What is it you do?'

Lassner scoffed. 'I am an art dealer.'

Arno thought back to the biography he'd been sent, back to his alter-ego contained in the letter. It mentioned that he himself was now connected to an art dealership.

'I have a gallery on Mulackstrasse,' the old man went on. 'We have many clients and some of them hold senior positions in the Party. One of them is Herr Göring.'

'Göring likes art?'

'Oh yes, he is a great art lover. Morphine and art. They are his two weaknesses.'

Arno knew he had to take the plunge. 'As fate would have it, I'm in the art trade too.'

'Really? What field are you in exactly?'

Arno wasn't prepared for the question and quickly sidetracked the conversation. 'Do you fancy a cognac with your coffee?'

'Why not? Waiter,' Lassner called, signalling to the hotel staff. 'Two cognacs please.'

As they waited for the drinks, Arno quickly thought over his next move, some way to exploit his connection to Göring and the Party. He had to get Lassner to trust him.

Their drinks were brought to the table as Arno started up again. 'I've always had an interest in art. In recent months I've been working for my uncle's art business. It's an administrative post but what I really want to do is to curate. Maybe we could help each other?'

Lassner smirked, which made Arno think he'd pushed too soon with his unsubtly.

Then after a momentary pause, Lassner spoke. 'Herr Hiller, you are both polite and brash when required, just like the Nazis!'

'I can secure a letter of the highest recommendation – it would be externally verified,' Arno said thinking he could arrange it with the secret police.

Lassner then bent down to the small satchel he'd been carrying and from it brought out a book. He balanced the book on his legs and opened the pages, flicking through them as if trying to locate a particular passage. It seemed obvious to Arno that something premeditated was about to take place, and this put him on his guard.

'I'm not interested,' Lassner said firmly.

Arno sat back in his chair before Lassner went on.

'You will come to work for me. I don't need a letter. You can help hang the paintings and keep out the rabble. You will show our guests around and pay special attention to our senior clients from the Party.'

'Arno clinked Lassner's glass with his own.

'We'll get you ship-shape. Other people don't know much about art. Apart from Göring. He probably knows more than I do. But knowledge isn't everything.'

'Isn't it?'

'Bluster! Bluster counts just as much. Can you feign enthusiasm? If you want to sound knowledgeable about art, then you need to act like you have strong opinions about it.'

Arno suddenly felt on safe ground. He could do that. Give him a yarn to spin and he'll be just fine.

'There will be a plan for you, be in no doubt. You will be part of a bigger operation and it will start soon, mark my words.'

Arno didn't think about the old gent's cryptic comments and accepted the offer with a handshake.

'Just a word of advice,' Lassner said finishing off his cognac. 'There is something brewing in the upper ranks of the Party. A new ambition, if you will. The Nazis can have a rather demented quality about them, as if they have a surprise they can't wait to unleash on everyone. You should turn a deaf ear in such cases.'

'Of course,' Arno said, intent on sniffing out exactly those sorts of details.

Herr Lassner smiled, as he shuffled his false teeth into his jaw.

'When do we start this?' Arno asked.

'Here, this is for you.' Lassner handed over the book that was still on his knee.

Arno flicked through the pages. They were completely empty.

'You can fill it with notes and observations,' Lassner said, as the two men stood up. 'Bring a pencil. I'm going to teach you all you need to know, starting tomorrow.'

23

On the streets, the first ochre leaves had fallen from the lime trees that grew tall and magnificent across the city. The leaves lit up beneath his feet as the streetlamps caught their golden reflection.

Arno made his way back home to Hallesches Tor, south of the city centre. It was a mixed district, with pockets of wealth scattered among plenty of down-and-outs. The local pawnbroker was one of the busiest places in the area. He was just closing up for the day as Arno returned, removing the vast array of wristwatches, wedding rings and war medals from his window display.

Within twenty minutes, Arno was inside Café Kaiser. He'd missed the Brownshirts with their collection tins; now was the time of night when the saxophones and trumpets broke out. The red table-lamps were switched on and the singers began to perform.

He sat in a cushioned booth hidden within the black painted walls, under dirty chandeliers that later would sparkle with light, transforming the soot-coloured barroom into a dazzling diamond. He ordered a *Tschunk* cocktail and as he drank, memories of Monika seeped into his mind like a river that had burst its banks. He remembered her, the line of her shoulders, the covering of fine invisible hairs on her neck, the shape of her waist. Where was she? The question would not fade. What about the police, Hannah Baumer and her ugly side-kick? What did they know? What the hell were they hiding?

He was disgruntled that they seemed to hold all the cards. He had no address, nor a telephone number for them. The only way for him to contact them was through the grey postbox where he was supposed to deliver his findings to, the location of which he hadn't tracked down yet.

It was clear this wasn't the everyday city police he was dealing with. If he was going to find them, he was going to have to take to the same shadows as they inhabited, occupying the same invisible contours that they travelled. But at least now he had a route into the higher ranks of the Party. What he would find out and disclose to the Prussian Police would be his choice. After all, he didn't trust them or anyone else for that matter.

As the cocktails slowly filtered through his veins and warmed his insides, he felt as though the answers to his questions were only a glass or two away…

It was midnight by the time Arno made his way back to his apartment. When he got there, he found a man lurking around the entrance to his attic room. The stranger was stood on the fifth floor, leaning against a wall, half-disfigured by shadows and the flashing of a neon light from the landing window behind him. Arno assumed he was like many men you saw around Berlin, jobless and wife-less, with plenty of time on their hands. The city was full of these drifter-sorts who didn't know whether a life of idling was something to be feared or embraced.

Arno passed by the stranger at first, until the man spoke up.

'Herr Hiller?' he asked, at which Arno swung around. His eyes were misted by several *Tschunk* cocktails and his step was swaying. The man came forward. He was gaunt about the face, with a pair of heavyset eyebrows and dimpled cheeks that caught shadows like the hollows of a tree.

As he emerged into the light, Arno saw he was nothing like the drifter he'd taken him to be. He wore a starched white collar strapped around his neck and the two corners folded forward like the wings of a moth. A dark grey jacket fitted him well, with white shirt sleeves poking out of the arms at a precise margin. He had three pens lined up in the breast pocket of his jacket. Under his arm, he carried a parcel. It was covered in brown paper; rectangular, about the size of an edition of the *Berliner Tageblatt* newspaper.

'This is for you.' The man offered the parcel. Arno cautiously took it. It weighed little more than a Spanish guitar. With its brown wrapping, it reminded him immediately of the painting presented to Göring at the lecture hall earlier.

'What's inside?'

The man in the starched collar told him that he'd been commissioned to create the object, and that once he'd finished, he should deliver it to this address.

'Who requested it?' Arno asked.

'That's classified,' the man said. 'You're just the recipient.'

Arno began to pull away the wrapping to unveil a painting.

'I've personally made this,' the stranger said with more than a touch of pride.

'You're an artist?' Arno responded.

'Actually, I prefer to think of myself as more of a businessman. Art is a mug's game.'

'Then why did you paint it?'

The man didn't seem to like this question. His eyes

dropped to the floor and he began rubbing his chin. Then he said, 'I've got more skill than any artist I've ever met.' He gave a sly look from the corners of his eyes. 'It takes real genius to do what I do.'

'And what's that then?'

The stranger held up his hands and began to inspect the end of his fingers. 'These aren't just the fingers of an artist. Any idiot can paint a pretty picture. These are the fingers of a virtuoso.'

'Is that so?'

'Why don't you take a look inside?'

Arno pulled back more of the paper. He knew little about art or the difference between a good painting and a bad one. Still, the image was a startling one. It showed a young boy with a great bouffant of brown hair and a strange, frightened expression on his face. His arm was recoiled, his bare shoulder squeezed up against his neck. Looking more closely, Arno could see the hand of the boy was recoiling from being bitten by what looked like a lizard jumping up from a bunch of grapes. It was one of the strangest things he'd ever seen.

'What if I told you that this painting is worth two hundred thousand marks?' the man asked.

'This? I'd be astonished – and suspicious.'

'Well, that's what I could sell it for if I wanted to.'

Arno looked at the object again. 'But instead you're giving it to me?'

The man's eyes opened wide and seemed to sparkle a little. 'You think it's stolen don't you? You think I'm a common thief?'

'I think it's strange that you're so happy to part with it if it's worth so much money.'

'Why don't you turn it over,' the man said.

On the rear side of the painting was a sheet of typed paper fixed with tape. The paper was titled with a single word: 'Provenance'. The text below listed names and places, most of them Italian in their sounding. Cardinal so-and-so from Rome, Principessa so-and-so from Naples. Arno's eyes skimmed over the list.

'What is this?'

The stranger explained it was a record of previous owners. 'That list is supposed to prove where the painting came from. That's what historians like to get hold of, so they can be sure of the journey the object has taken. It's meant to be proof of authenticity. In my opinion, the painting itself is convincing enough.'

Arno understood. 'This is a fake, isn't it? A forgery, with this fabricated history of owners?'

'You catch on pretty quick, don't you?'

Arno's head was beginning to clear. He knew he had to get to grips with the object.

'It's a Caravaggio,' the stranger said. 'It's called *Boy Bitten by a Lizard*.'

'Caravaggio?' It was faintly familiar – the artist's name.

'He's Italian. Very well-known, if you know your art.'

'So you make forgeries for the police. And now I'm supposed to use this to get close to the people in the Party?'

'Don't ask me. Make some money with it if you want or just show it off. That's what most of my clients do. They like to parade like peacocks. Come into my study and see my Rubens, they say. It's all about out-ranking each other. As I said, it's a mug's game.'

Arno looked at the object and began to perceive the possibility for the painting. It would be his way into the higher ranks of the Nazi Party via Lassner's gallery, a badge of honour as he entered the world of selling art.

He wanted to quiz the art forger further on what it all meant, but as soon as he thought this he realised the man was already descending the staircase. Arno called after him but he was already on the floor below and trickling downwards at a pace. Arno waited a few moments, then went up to his attic room carrying the canvas under his arm.

He began to think back to his undercover identity as described in the paperwork from the police. He went straight to the written biography and focussed on a particular passage with the following words:

'I have established myself as an art dealer with a special interest in the civil and moral status of Jews in German society. Many great works of art lie within the private collections of Jewish families across Europe and are also subject to the Jewish question. I have made it my purpose to liberate these paintings from the clutches of Jewish collectors for the greater public good and the cultural benefit of the German people.'

As Arno read the passage he began to take note of its peculiar thrust, its defiant tone dressed up in a moral purpose. It rang out clearly; and the painting in his possession bolstered his position. He took the police dossier to the sink and struck a match, letting the flame catch hold of the file.

He then wrapped the forged painting back up in the brown paper and slid the parcel beneath his bed. As he lay back on his lumpy mattress, the spiral of events took him back to Monika. He hoped desperately she was okay and couldn't wait to get started with Lassner the next day.

24

Early next morning Arno took a tram to Mulackstrasse, clutching the wrapped-up painting under his arm. He'd dressed up as best he could. He had a special pair of shoes his parents had given him, ones he would have saved for an important day in his life, like marrying Monika or going to his mother's funeral. Today was important enough, he decided. He looked down at his dark green Brogues with their laces fashionably set to one side, their brightly coloured stitching and short floppy tassels.

As he walked, the Berlin rain attacked him from every direction. By the time he arrived at the gallery, the shoes, along with the paper parcel, were temporarily pockmarked with damp.

Then he noticed the window of the gallery. It had a sign saying '*Neue Sachlichkeit Kunst*' – New Objectivity Art. With his head spinning from the night before, he pushed open the door to get inside and begin. A lady greeted him. She was middle-aged, had arching eyebrows and was wearing a dress with small black stars printed on the fabric. In her hair, she had a large pin in the shape of what looked like a swallow or a house martin.

'I'm here to see Herr Lassner.'

'Do you have an appointment?' she asked politely.

'No, but he is expecting me.'

'Herr Lassner has had to leave the premises for a short time,' came the reply. 'But you are welcome to look around our new exhibition.' She handed him a diagrammatic guide to the current show. Her mascara laden eyes and vivid red lipstick gave her away: highly-educated, enterprising, expectant of great things in her life and confident she would achieve them. He was happy to meet her; perhaps she would be showing him the ropes later and teaching him all about art.

With an outstretched arm she directed him towards a pair of opaque glass doors that slid open on invisible wheels, parting in a smooth, modern way. On the other side of the glass were paintings by some two-dozen German artists.

Arno looked around, checking over the interior of the gallery. The walls were wide and painted white. The pictures hung from long metal wires hooked to a rail just below the ceiling. He observed there were several curtained doorways that led off from the main gallery room – it made sense to him to make a note of the layout. There was a velvet covered armchair in one corner, and next to it an ashtray on a chrome stand. He wondered what security there was, and if the Nazis met in the open space of the gallery or whether there was some private quarter that they utilised.

The brightly coloured paintings hung in their simple dark-wood frames like lanterns in winter, intense packets of colour along a snowdrift of white wall.

Arno toured in silence. He became distracted when he found he was no longer alone in the gallery. His companion for the exhibition was a tall, well-dressed man with narrow shoulders and a particular way of stooping in front of every painting for prolonged periods. Arno could only see the back of his head. He moved about quietly and precisely, shifting from one picture to the next as if the strange gallery step was highly cultivated in him.

After a while, Arno began to notice an odd thing about the stranger: that he liked to stand extremely close to the paintings. So close, his face was sometimes less than an inch from the canvas. Daringly close, Arno thought for such priceless objects. If he sneezed he would certainly be arrested for vandalism!

Their rhythm around the gallery was unintentionally matched. Every time Arno tried to walk in the opposite direction, the other man seemed to walk in that direction too. His shoes, two glistening bullets rubbed almost golden about the toe, clopped loudly across the floor. Arno's soft-soled shoes trailed shortly after, with the pad and peel of rubber on the slick gallery floor.

It was only after a while that Arno realised that the man was familiar. When he turned, he recognised him instantly. It was the distinguished-looking soldier from Café Bauer, the one he was watching when he was with Käthe and Thomas. He was dressed in military uniform that day. Today he wore civilian clothing. But it was unmistakably him. Most of all, it was the proud, confident expression that gave him away. The lights in the gallery revealed it; as he turned to face Arno, his noble arrogance rang out like a bell.

Arno turned his attention to the paintings around the room and began to see more clearly what they depicted. He had expected to find picturesque countryside scenes and portraits of old German barons or something to that effect. Instead, the paintings were far more modern. They showed bawdy jazz bars with venal-looking men counting money, prostitutes murdered with knives, old naked lovers in wrinkled embraces, doctors holding up sinister syringes, war-wounded men on homemade crutches, people with big yellow teeth and hairy warts on their chins, and lots of people smoking. And, most of all, there was a great deal of nudity. It was really quite a peculiar and disturbing selection of paintings. Grotesque, extreme and raw.

The Nazi in the gallery seemed especially animated with the details. Every time he went in close, he glared at the naked organs, fixing his attention on all the most flesh-rich passages with intense and vigorous interest.

Arno placed him at about forty years old. He was smartly turned out in the respectable bourgeois dress. He had blue eyes and a prideful way of holding his head up high. Or it might have been mere disdain, barely concealed, for when he looked across at Arno, he gave a surly, hostile expression.

Finally, they reached the last painting in the room where the exhibition came to an end. It was then that Herr Lassner arrived from behind one of the curtains; and as the Nazi left, he and Arno shot glances at each other one last time.

25

'That was one of our prestigious clients,' were Lassner's first whispered words. 'That man. He's usually here with Göring, but he comes from time to time on his own too.'

'Who is he?'

Lassner's eyes lit up. 'His name is Count Hermann Graf von Hessen. Or Hessen for short. He's an aristocrat turned general. You remember the Brownshirts from the meeting yesterday? He's their leader in Berlin. Hitler recruited him to make an army out of that fine stock of men.'

'I saw him a couple of days ago in Café Bauer.'

Lassner smiled, his false teeth sliding to one side. 'Yes, he likes to socialise. In public too. The elitist life. No shame.'

'No shame?'

'I don't say it offensively, just that he's rather bold in not holding back. He prefers to live extrovertly. Gambling. Horses. Even boys – that's not unusual in today's Berlin of course.'

'And he likes art too, by the looks of it.'

'He's acquired quite a few pieces in the past, when the money is flowing. These days he's more tight-fisted but he still comes in to view the paintings. He likes the nudes especially.'

'Yes I noticed,' Arno said.

'He's always like that. Art is another form of indulgence for him but he's still a respected client. His main purpose here is for the Party meetings.'

Arno's ears pricked up. 'So the gallery has some affiliation with the Party then?'

'Only as a matter of utmost discretion.'

'As a fellow supporter, I'll observe that.'

Lassner stared at Arno for a moment. 'Come with me.'

Herr Lassner led Arno through a door and into a back room. He pulled aside a tapestry curtain to reveal a metal door. It led into a second room, which had the feel of some sort of annexe. There was a ceramic sink in the corner, and in the middle of the room, a wooden table with three glass ashtrays on it.

'This is where they congregate and do their business. I've seen all sorts around this table. Göring. Hessen. Röhm. Others. Never Hitler, mind you.'

'What do they do here?'

'I'm not sure. The door is guarded and I'm not allowed inside most of the time.'

'So your role is as Göring's art dealer?'

'In a manner of speaking. I protect his interests. Now, what have we got here?' Lassner spotted the parcel beneath Arno's arm. 'Looks like you've brought me a gift.'

Arno lifted the parcel onto the table and began to peel away the paper. Lassner became fixated. He opened a table drawer and took out a silver magnifying glass and hovered the lens above the canvas. He sniffed the surface, then examined at the edges before returning to the front again, holding it at arm's length.

'Impressive,' he nodded, his eyes flicking left and right. 'This is very good. Whoever did this is very talented.'

'It's genuine,' Arno said, trying his luck. 'It's the real thing.'

Lassner glanced across at him. 'You'll have to do better than that.'

Arno scratched his head.

'It's excellent. Truly. It's one of the best I've seen. But you must think, why would someone in your position be in possession of such a valuable object like this? You'll have to sound more commanding, if you understand my meaning.'

Arno thought for a moment. 'This exceptional piece is a rare find. Its authenticity is confirmed by an impeccable record of ownership.'

'That's more convincing. Let's keep going. Why don't you tell me who the artist is? It looks Italian to me.'

'Yes, that's right. Italian.'

'How old is it?'

'I thought I'd let you decide.'

'Try late sixteenth century. And the artist?'

'The artist's name is Caravaggio.'

'Good work. We'll have you dealing in no time.' Lassner examined the painting once more. He seemed oddly excited by the object, his old face taking on a sprightly look. 'We'll find a safe place for this. When the time comes, we'll have to make a big show of it. You'll have to be prepared. There'll be no second chances.'

26

Arno's initiation into buying and selling art went straight into the thick of it. It consisted of multiple tours of the works of art hung on display in the gallery. Lassner took the initiate around every single painting and made statements about each one with a rather cool, businesslike slant.

'This one is by Ernst Kirchner. German by birth. He tends to appeal to the cosmopolitan type. Two thousand marks for him, if the right person walks through that door.'

Onto the next.

'Karl Hubbuch. Almost impossible to sell. Don't know why we bother. But I rather like him.'

And again.

'Otto Dix. Prefers the savage side of life, but is surprisingly popular. Six thousand marks for this painting on a good day.'

After a couple of hours, Arno realised that these brief injunctions were just the start of his training in the selling of paintings. Lassner brought out a selection of books and set them aside for him to read through the week. As for the paintings on display, Lassner rarely spoke about their subject directly, except in relation to the market.

'This one. Slevogt. Only ever painted outdoors. For a

work this size, fifteen-hundred marks. Nineteen-hundred if the wind is in our favour.'

There was however one painting that Lassner seemed to show an emotional response to. It hung in his office room at the back of the gallery. When Arno asked about it, the art dealer's expression softened. 'This is perhaps my favourite and isn't for sale. It's by our very own Caspar Friedrich from Greifswald. Early nineteenth century. It is melancholy, yes, but spiritual. He was a painter alive to God's presence in every rock, tree and sunrise.'

The image was of a series of boats on a body of water, cast into silhouettes by a purple sunset.

'When it's time for my retirement, I'll sell this if I need to. It should keep me in robust finances for a decade at least. I've even taken the insurance of getting Herr Göring to verify the painting for me, in case there's any doubt over the authenticity. I'm thinking ahead, you see.'

Arno spent the rest of the day delving into the books he'd been given and educating himself about art and its history. He had to try and pass as an expert. Using the books, he started to search for some of the paintings in the gallery. He learned words like 'composition', '*contrapposto*' and 'Renaissance'. He committed these words to memory, determined he could make good use of them when the time came.

Late in the day, as he stood duty over the gallery reception, a lady came in through the door. She wore a big heavy dress with ruffles and lace, as if she'd just stepped in from the last century. She paused to look at a painting for about a second, then turned to Arno to make her intentions patently clear: 'I'm here to buy something,' she said, passing her eyes around the full panorama of the room.

'Okay let's try this,' Arno thought to himself.

'What kind of style are you looking for?' He said, rising from behind the desk to accompany the woman. He felt ready for a splash of bluster.

She was immediately on the back foot. 'Oh, I don't know. How should I? Most pictures I see, I don't like. Show me what you have.'

Her manner was impatient, a touch haughty. He led her to a nearby picture.

'What do you think of this piece?'

'Think?'

'Is it interesting?'

'No, it's awful. I just see a scrawl. What is it?'

'It's by a painter from Dortmund.'

'No, no, no. There's nothing to it. Show me something else. Quickly.'

He took her to a different section of the gallery where three paintings were hung on the wall in a row. 'If I were to ask you which of these you liked the most, which one would you select?' he said, adopting a change of tactics.

Now the lady began to think, considering each alternative very closely. She seemed to prefer this way of shopping. She squinted at the wall and looked at the works carefully. Arno stood beside her pretending to gaze at the paintings along with her. Eventually, she stepped forward and raised her finger to point at the painting in the middle.

'This one. I like this one the best. Don't ask me why. I can't justify it. Just my taste, that's all.'

'A fine choice.'

'Fine choice? Tell me, why is it a fine choice?'

'It's a city landscape. The composition is excellent. The colours are Renaissance style. The harmony is wonderful.'

'Is that so? Which city is it?'

'Somewhere in Italy, perhaps.' Then, he suspected this was too vague – 'A rare view of Florence,' he corrected. 'From an unusual angle. Most original.'

'Is it? How about that. Florence. I wouldn't have recognised it. I've always wanted to go to Florence.'

'This artist takes his imagery from his upbringing and his memories, so we can assume he is a painter of deepest expression.'

'We can assume that, can we?'

'We can conjecture, yes. This piece is by Oswald Achenbach.'

The lady stood quietly for a moment, digesting what had been said. 'What is the price?'

'It is priced at 7,000 marks,' Arno replied, choosing to exaggerate.

'Isn't that a bit dear?'

'It is the market value for this artist at the moment.'

'In that case I'll leave it.'

'It has attracted interest from other patrons. It may not be on display for much longer.'

'Like I said, I'm not interested.'

'Damn,' Arno muttered, as the woman walked out of the gallery.

Lassner then entered the room. 'Was that your first client?'

'She was.'

'Did you manage to share any information with her about our paintings?'

'Yes, it went okay until…'

'Until what?'

'The mention of the price. I inflated it slightly, thinking I could hustle her.'

Lassner looked disappointed. 'That isn't a good start. You need to learn to walk before you run. I would leave the discussion over cost to me,' he said, failing to hide his irritation.

Arno gritted his teeth. 'Of course.' He almost couldn't help bartering with the woman. It is what he'd done in his previous line of *work*. But he realised this was a completely different setup and he had to play by the book or at least appear to.

He continued to study the gallery books with few other visitors that afternoon. Then ten minutes before closing was due, he heard the gallery doorbell ring. Lassner went to unbolt the doors to find a lady eager to get inside. Arno started packing up his things in the small staffroom when he heard a familiar voice. He wandered into the gallery room to find Lassner in incessant conversation with the same lady from earlier that afternoon.

'Here is the gentleman who assisted me earlier,' she said to Lassner. 'I've decided to buy the painting after all. That was a good tip you gave me earlier,' she said turning to Arno.

'Glad I was of service.' Arno looked at Lassner, who maintained a serious expression.

At this juncture, Lassner called the lady into his back office and a price for the painting was discussed. Arno left the negotiations to the proprietor. After the lady had left, agreeing to collect the painting later that week, Lassner approached his new novice. 'It seems you were lucky this time.'

'Maybe,' Arno said, concealing his sense of satisfaction.

'Ha!' Lassner then clicked his fingers. 'You've done better than you think. Actually, I can't believe it!'

'What do you mean?'

'That lady is visiting from out of town and her husband is an investor, with a particular interest in future art speculations. She told him about the Achenbach painting and he has predicted that its worth will multiply two-fold in the next few years.'

'But you'll lose its future value won't you?'

'No, because the price you gave her is already twice its value. We'll cash in before it generates its predicted worth and if it doesn't we've made a handsome profit anyway!'

'Why would they buy it for a higher value when it's currently worth less?'

'It must be seen as a low risk and her husband must be sure he will capitalise on it.'

'Even with the state of the German economy?'

'It may be unstable but not for the elite.'

Arno grinned at the result of his gamble. 'I stuck to the paintings I read about today. Then I wanted to try my hand at a dose of bluster, just as you said!'

'Well, you've set the bar high having sold your first work. Now, there's no going back.'

27

At the end of Arno's second day, Lassner announced tomorrow's prospective guest.

'What's he like?' Arno asked.

'Göring? He's forthright and likes the good life. Brought up in the true German style. Castles in the mountains, hunting in the forests, that sort of thing. You'll see when he comes. A Bavarian beast, with all the finery to match. Just look at his hands, all the gold rings he wears. Those rubies are real, let me assure you. He even designs his own uniforms. He likes to think he's set apart.'

'And he's an art collector?'

'Yes, among other things – he collects art. He collects jewels and lavish articles. He imbibes whatever is put in front of him. Someone once told me he keeps a baby tiger as a pet. In short, he doesn't say no to many things.'

After the news of Göring's visit, Arno took himself to the backroom with a packet of cigarettes and an armful of art books. He would spend all night studying them if it meant that he could return tomorrow armed with some art talk. To meet Göring face to face was a chance too good to miss – so he would make sure he was ready for it.

The next morning, Arno was waiting by the opaque

glass doors of the gallery when a small entourage of men arrived. First among them was Hermann Göring himself. He wore a pale, dove-blue military uniform that wrapped tightly around his belly like a body in a hammock. With him were two other men; one of them carried a briefcase and wore a sharply tailored suit, the other was dressed in the customary brown uniform, black boots and circular kepi cap.

They arrived in high spirits, smiling between them and sharing a joke. Göring had the eminent confidence of someone who was used to being listened to. He led the way, walking directly past Arno, who chose not to draw attention just yet. His moment would come soon enough.

The three visitors took a few moments to examine some of the paintings hung on the walls. They played the game of trying to sound knowledgeable and astute. There was the distinct air of competitiveness between them; a sport that, in the end, no one would let Göring lose.

Göring went ahead and began a private conversation with Lassner, shaking his hand and patting him on the shoulder. They were very familiar with each other and obviously had a trusting friendship. At this point, Lassner called Arno over to be introduced. Arno approached, feeling a shimmer of nerves ripple through him.

Lassner introduced Arno as his *protégé*. Göring seemed to enjoy the idea. He smiled, that strange sickle smile, like the shape of a crescent moon or a scorpion arching its back. Then there was a moment of silence, and it was obvious that Arno was meant to fill it. Off the top of his head, he began to talk about some of the famous artists he'd read about the night before. The words seem to come to him easily, as if the pressure of the moment – his great need to impress Göring – was squeezing the thoughts out of him, words propelled by his hidden motives.

He had to seize the opportunity that was presenting itself. It was time to mention the Caravaggio. With his best poise – eyes wide, head tall – he turned to Göring and said in a tone of intimacy, 'I have recently acquired a piece that I feel may be of interest to you.'

Göring replied casually, 'Have you now?'

Arno made his play unambiguously. 'I have made it my business to procure works of art from the Jewish community. Like many others, I'm concerned that great treasures sit in the wrong hands. Art is like anything precious: without the proper attention, it can be taken for granted. This particular painting I was able to liberate from a desperate family who – typically for these people – had let greed overtake their basic needs. The work is by the great Italian, Caravaggio. I believe you are an admirer.'

Göring nodded. 'Italian artists, I do admire their sense of style. Caravaggio? We'll see.'

'Can I have a word?' Lassner prompted lightly, catching Arno's eye.

Arno went with him to the other side of the room whilst Göring watched on, amused by this need for a tête-à-tête.

'I'm not sure this is the right time,' Lassner said tentatively. 'The other gent over there, that's Göring's personal art adviser. He's not much of a businessman, but he has a fierce eye for detail. He's something of an art fanatic and what he doesn't know about Italian painting is not worth knowing.'

'But we have the painting here. Why wait?' Arno replied.

'All I am saying is this: the information you have, it better be good. If there's a hole in your story, he will spot it. If it sounds even slightly irregular, he's bound to suspect.'

'So, may we see the painting or not?' Göring called over, intentionally interrupting.

Lassner returned to his guest, stuffy with apologies. By now, Göring had been joined by his adviser; both were waiting in anticipation, as if a sold-out show at the Wintergarten Variety Theatre was about to begin. 'I've been sharing the news of this recent discovery,' Göring said. 'We are growing more intrigued by the minute.'

'Is it possible to see the Caravaggio?' the adviser asked more formally. His voice was rough and hoarse, like he needed to clear his throat – which he never did.

Arno roused himself and spoke up. He realised the only way to get through this was with guts. 'It's in the back room. You can see it right away.'

Lassner, returning to his role as gallery owner, showed not the least hint of objection. He smiled and led the way, taking them through doorways to the gallery's private quarters. They assembled in the back room around the wooden table and switched on the overhead light. Lassner fetched the painting and laid it down on the table for the group to scrutinise.

'*Boy Bitten by a Lizard*,' Arno declared, introducing the painting in the grandest tone he could muster.

After a moment's pause to glance over the work, Göring spoke first. 'It has no frame,' he said frowning. 'It looks naked.'

'Not every work comes to us in a fully prepared form,' Lassner replied. 'It is for people like you and me to cherish the object within, not merely how it's dressed up.'

Göring nodded, quietly agreeing with Lassner's advice.

Arno was impressed with the way Lassner had

guided the politician towards a better perspective. He took the lead. 'I managed to acquire the painting in fleeting circumstances. The truth is, many families are on the move presently and their possessions find themselves in transit. This is how I take my advantage. When a family is on the back-foot, they tend to be more willing to agree to my terms.'

'So the painting belonged to a Jewish family?' Göring's adviser asked.

'To an Austrian family who are at this very moment sailing towards the United States. The proceeds of this painting have helped fund their passage from Europe. Of course, I achieved a very favourable price for the object, but because of circumstances, it did not include the frame.'

The adviser now proceeded to pick up the canvas and hold it up at various angles. From his pocket he took out a monocle and pressed it onto his eye. Then with the tips of his fingers, he lightly ran them over the surface of the painting. As he did, he uttered a single word: 'Provenance?'

'Its history is beyond doubt. The painting first belonged to a Roman dignitary by the name of Cardinal di Ripetta. It later passed onto the hands of the artist Guido Reni from the Bolognese School, acquired from the cardinal in payment for a private debt. Several generations later, inherited by a distant niece Francesco Savelli, she sold it to a Neapolitan family named Brigandi. Then it descended through the Brigandi family, who moved to Austria in the second half of the last century. There it stayed until finally, it came into my possession.'

Göring's attendant listened as he ranged his monocled eye in and out across the painting. Arno's explanatory speech was delivered perfectly and met with nods of understanding.

'So, what do we think?' Göring asked, stepping up and taking the item from his adviser.

The adviser popped out the monocle from his eye and said slowly, 'It's good. It's very good. It is fake, of course.'

'Yes, of course.' Göring said.

'It's a very good fake, but a fake nonetheless. All the usual signs are there.'

'All the signs are there,' Göring repeated gloatingly.

Arno passed an uncertain glance to Lassner, who in return responded with a less-than discreet wince.

'Gentlemen, please, it's not possible to describe an object such as this as a fake,' Lassner said, stumbling over his response. 'It's just not possible, may I say. It's more than perplexing, and if I may add, rather offensive, that you could think –' Lassner began running his fingertips along the edge of the table in a frustrated pendulum fashion.

Now Arno took up the defence. 'As I explained, we can trace the work back through many generations of owners, back through the centuries, all the way to its origins. To the very hand of Caravaggio.'

'We have little else to say on the matter,' Göring said.

'This is a great opportunity,' Arno replied. 'You're making a mistake.'

Lassner interrupted. 'No, no. Our guests do not make mistakes.'

'But, they're wrong –'

Lassner put his hand on Arno's wrist. 'No more,' he said firmly.

All eyes turned to Göring, whose expression changed in an instant. His stare was cold and unblinking. 'Mistake?' he said finally, his face hardly moving. He looked at Arno with a fearsomeness that Arno had never seen in anybody before. His great frame and wide face formed a single looming edifice.

Inside, Arno felt himself wavering – and at the same time, he wanted to resist being beaten. 'Perhaps our guest would like to reconsider?' he suggested back to Lassner.

Now the room of four men fell silent. Lassner shook his head. The adviser turned away as if he couldn't stand to watch what might happen next. Göring locked eyes with Arno, who in return, stared back unrelentingly.

'You silly people,' Göring said eventually, booming loudly. 'We have deceived you – this is our idea of a joke!' He gave a lilting, high-pitched laugh. 'How else could we attempt to flush you out if not with a bit of horseplay?'

Göring and his adviser swapped great quivering grins between them. Their delight was overbearing. Arno and Lassner looked at each other, allowing themselves an awkward smile. Then Göring immediately changed from his humourous mood to a serious tone. 'It's a wonderful piece, but I'm afraid we are not interested. A very fine work of art, I won't argue about that. I possess many priceless artworks,' he said boastfully, 'most of them from supposedly persecuted Jews but this isn't one for my collection. We're not interested.'

Arno hid his disappointment.

'However,' Göring went on, 'I must congratulate you on your project, young man. There's a great deal of nonsense spoken in defence of the Jewish people. What their defenders fail to see is that the German people would be altogether more successful if we could be liberated from the clutches of their manipulation. I let others put it into theory, but action – yes, that is something I can appreciate. Young men like you, taking the initiative, taking steps like this, rehabilitating our cultural heirlooms, it's all to be applauded.'

Göring smiled, his strange slivering lips widening and separating like the mouth of some alien fish. Arno bowed to his compliment as he wondered what to do next. Convincing Göring to buy the painting would have won him favour. But it seemed too late to get him to change his mind.

The entourage of men left the gallery a short time later, after Göring had signed some paperwork for Lassner and made a private telephone call.

Then, as they passed into the street, Göring turned to Arno and said, 'Young man, make yourself available tomorrow. I'll send a car for you at midday. There's someone I want you to meet.'

28

That night, as Arno journeyed home, he realised the situation had turned to his benefit. He had persuaded Göring and his adviser that the painting was genuine. That in itself was an achievement. He didn't know what lay in store tomorrow but his deception had to remain tight.

Just then, as he was stepping off the tram at Hallesches Tor a short distance from his apartment, he felt a presence lurking behind him. He turned to find Monika's father bearing down at a pace.

'Where is my daughter?' came his angry voice.

Arno was taken aback. Why was he here? Was there news about Monika?

'I said, where's my daughter?'

'I don't know,' Arno replied quickly.

'You must know something.'

Herr Goldstein grabbed Arno by his shirt collar and pushed him against a wall. The turn of violence took Arno by surprise. Herr Goldstein brought his face so near that their noses were almost touching. His face was unshaven, his stubble a great gloom of darkness across his cheeks and jawline.

'Herr Goldstein, what is this?'

'She was supposed to come home three nights ago. She told us she was going on a theatre trip, but we haven't seen her since. None of her friends know where she is. We've been everywhere. And none of them have heard anything about an excursion either.'

'I'm sorry. I have no idea where she is.' Arno felt a layer of sweat prickle on his forehead. He managed to push Herr Goldstein away but only for a moment.

'You're lying to me. I know it. You're the only friend of hers I haven't spoken to.'

'I don't know where she is any more than you do.'

Monika's father tightened his grip on Arno's collar. Arno could feel a rack of bony knuckles pressing into his collar bone. When he glanced down, he saw a row of thick fingers screwed into his chest. If it was anyone else he wouldn't put up with it but in these circumstances he was reluctant to fight back.

'Her mother is worried sick,' Herr Goldstein went on. 'Something like this will make her ill. We are going out of our minds. I'm telling you, if you know something about where our daughter is, you better tell me now. God forbid…'

'She'll turn up, she's level-headed,' Arno said, basing his conjecture on the hope he would find or liberate her somehow soon.

She had actually been missing for five days now, not just the three as Herr Goldstein believed. But Arno's words seemed to have a sobering effect on him. His grip eased, and he became suddenly self-conscious, stepping back and brushing himself down, as if aware of being out in public and that someone he might know could be watching.

He had the look of a man who was used to restraining himself, perhaps someone who worried over things too much and became agitated all too easily, who then had to rein himself in to save face. He had none of the noble serenity of their previous meeting, when Arno had seen him stood tall before his fireplace, like an assured monarch in his own castle. Now he carried a dangerous unrest, a common man's dismay. It vibrated all through him like a simmering pot that might boil over at any minute.

Arno stood back against the wall, his eyes pinned on the figure in front of him. Now Herr Goldstein began digging around in his jacket pocket. He handed Arno an envelope.

'What's this?'

'Read it,' Herr Goldstein said.

Arno pulled open the flap and took out a folded letter.

'Read it aloud,' Herr Goldstein instructed.

Arno began reading. '*We have taken your daughter.*' He glanced up at Monika's father and then back down at the letter. The writing was hard to make out. It was typed in letters that were oddly spaced out and uneven. He read on. '*If you ever want to see your daughter alive again, then you'll have to pay fifty-thousand marks ransom.*' He scrunched the edges of the letter in disbelief and suspicion. 'This suggests that Monika has been kidnapped.'

'That's exactly what it says.'

'But' – Arno began calculating the hours and days since he'd last seen her. What time did he wake up in the hotel room? How long did he spend looking for her in that dusty old town?

'Keep reading,' Herr Goldstein said.

Arno continued. The letter explained that the kidnappers intended to phone the Goldsteins at three o'clock in the afternoon. He read on. '*When you answer the phone, simply tell us you will pay the ransom. If you call the police or if you do not pay, we will kill your daughter.*'

'It can't be right,' Arno said beginning to pace, unable to hide his anguish.

'We haven't seen Monika since she left last Friday. This letter presented itself yesterday morning. There's no postmark.'

'Did you get the phone call?'

'Yes, at exactly three o'clock yesterday. We answered. Nobody spoke.'

'What did you say?'

'We said we'd pay, of course. What else could we say?'

Arno was at a loss. Had she really been taken during the short time he was out? Was it true or was this letter part of the ploy to force him into working for the police?

Seeing Monika's father distraught, he decided to share a shred of truth. 'I believe Monika has been with a friend this weekend,' he said boldly.

Herr Goldstein looked up, his face locked with a fresh irritation. 'What?'

'It's supposed to be a secret.'

'What do you mean?'

'She has met someone. She has an admirer.' As the words left his mouth, he felt a cruel sting of self-betrayal. To conceal his own existence like that meant gritting his teeth. But then he remembered his assignment and realised that it was prudent to play the role.

Herr Goldstein shook his head, not knowing whether to be relieved or enraged. 'I don't believe it. How do you know all this?'

'She confided in me.'

'What about this letter?'

'Somebody is taunting you. It's a horrible hoax – a sick joke.'

Herr Goldstein considered Arno's explanation, knowing how cruel and hostile people could be. 'We've forbidden Monika from having a boyfriend. Not without our knowledge anyway. What is his name? Where does he live?'

Arno had an automatic urge to glance up at his own building. They were at the exact spot where Herr Goldstein would march to if he knew who the boyfriend really was. He resisted, saying instead, 'He's not from around here. He's from Hamburg, I think.'

'Hamburg?' Herr Goldstein seemed to consider the logistics of travelling north. 'Is that where they are now?'

'I don't know. Probably.'

'This is intolerable.' Goldstein looked up and down the street as if searching for a sign that would tell him what to say or think next. He turned back to Arno. 'If you hear from her, you must let me know. Immediately. If Monika is not home by the end of today, I'll hold you personally responsible. Do you comprehend my meaning?'

'Yes,' Arno answered abruptly. 'I understand.'

Herr Goldstein gave Arno a stern look before marching off in the direction from which he came – nearly coming face-to-face with a passing tram as he crossed the street. Boyfriend or not, he wanted his daughter back home. Back where she belonged.

29

Arno sat in bed that night and tried to fathom the series of events, beginning in the hotel room where he'd been lying with Monika through to Herr Goldstein brandishing the kidnapper's letter. It all felt like a farce, as if some satirical game was being played without his knowledge. And yet the facts remained as they were: Monika was still missing and no one had seen or heard from her in days. And now, there was this explanation.

With a dreadful sense of foreboding, he began to remember stories he used to hear from compatriots in the party, about the prospect of raising funds by blackmail and kidnap. At the time they'd seemed to be rumour more than anything. Still, the idea tended to circulate between the excitable younger members – teenagers like himself – who got a kick out of the thought that not only could it be an easy method of extorting cash, but that a family – especially a Jewish one – might suffer along the way

He began to picture Monika as the victim of one of these plots. The image that crystallised in his mind saw her in the soft light of his fondest memories. It was the face of the girl he loved. He thought of her being stolen away from the city, bundled into a vehicle, perhaps tied up with a cover over her head, escorted like an animal to some dirty, anonymous hideaway. The idea quickly sparked a desire to smash something against the wall in front of him. Then his mind slipped onto the question of her kidnappers and immediately his imagination swarmed with even darker images, of a stranger's hands gripping her, by force and maltreatment, and of her face crippled in fright. It was all too terrible to envisage…

He woke the following morning after a restless night, feeling backed into a corner. Even if he was able to reach the Prussian Police and ask them about the ransom note, they still had the upper hand. The stage was unpredictable and the only thing he could move towards right now was exposing Vendetta.

The personal invitation Göring had given him, to be at the gallery on Mulackstrasse at midday, awaited him. He went out onto the street where the morning was strumming with sunlight and the incessant rattle of passing traffic. He took a tram and crossed the city. With so little to go on, it felt like his only option was to forge ahead with his present duty. He felt wretched and wired but it was time to focus on the day ahead – a day he intended would bring him a step closer to Monika's recovery.

On the way to the gallery, he took a detour to the Goldstein's house. Monika's father had said he held him personally responsible if Monika hadn't returned home and in an untoward way it felt true. Having been accosted by her father, he thought he'd go to them to show initiative. Besides which, he wanted to know if there was any more news about Monika's abductors.

It was exactly nine o'clock in the morning as the tram pulled up at a junction in Schöneberg. He checked around that he wasn't being followed. Satisfied he was alone, he went on towards the Goldstein household. The local shoe-shiner was nowhere to be seen. Arno went up the stone steps where there were a pair of pots on either side of the door. The flowers in them had withered and died. He pulled the bell-ringer and waited.

As several minutes passed he noted the overall quietness of the house; it seemed unnaturally still. At the very least he expected a maid to come, even if Monika's parents were out. Then, from the corner of his eye, he saw a curtain blind twitch and a face appear furtively before it quickly vanished.

More minutes went by with Arno on the doorstep. A cat came up and rubbed its flank against his leg, gave a timid cry and then hopped beneath a nearby shrub. At last, the great door opened and the face of Herr Goldstein appeared.

'I've come to see if there's any more news,' Arno said, briskly walking through into the hallway. 'Has Monika returned?'

Herr Goldstein looked tired. Beyond him, Frau Goldstein stood in the hall, wringing her wrists with her hands.

'We've had a second letter,' Herr Goldstein said. His voice had a brittle, scratchy quality, like burnt charcoal.

'A second letter? What does it say?'

'You better come through.'

'We've not heard from our daughter,' said Frau Goldstein. She had no makeup on and her features were drawn and faded.

Herr Goldstein went into the drawing-room and motioned for Arno to follow. Monika's mother stood lingering in the doorway, preferring not to enter the room. Herr Goldstein moved to the study table and turned to address the visitor.

'Quite obviously, your story of Monika having a boyfriend was fabricated,' he said.

Arno skulked for a second, then immediately asked,

'May I see the second letter?'

Herr Goldstein picked up a piece of paper from the desk and handed it over. 'But for now we have to consider the facts in front of us.'

Arno read the letter. At once he felt its terrible power, like a tide of dirty water gathering around his legs and rising. It was the worst of objects. The kidnappers were insisting on payment, this time detailing the conditions of the exchange of money:

'So far, Monika is safe. To keep her that way, it is time to pay. We want the money in used 100-mark notes. It will be delivered inside a suitcase. The suitcase is to be taken to a location which we will inform you of by telephone, at a time of our choosing. Monika's father will drive alone in a brown car travelling at 20km/h. He will drop the suitcase from the car and will then drive on for half-a-mile. He will turn around and return. Monika will be despatched if the money is correct.'

Frau Goldstein stepped forward. Her fingers were trembling. 'We don't know what to do.'

Arno looked over at her in her distress. 'I'll help in any way I can,' he replied. He couldn't shake off his guilt over Monika's disappearance. 'Have you been to the police?'

Herr Goldstein glanced at his wife. 'I've spoken to some colleagues, people who know about the intricacies of such things. I've been strongly advised to hesitate before contacting the police. As the first letter stated, Monika will be in far greater danger if we involve them.'

'So you'll meet the conditions and pay the ransom?'

'We desperately want this to end. We want our daughter home as soon as possible. But the sum of money is out of our reach.'

Arno replied, more bluntly than he intended, 'How

so?'

'They must think we have more than we do,' Frau Goldstein said, still standing in the doorway.

Monika's father lowered his head, looking disappointed and aggrieved. A moment later he spoke frankly. 'We have next to nothing. That's all I can tell you. Virtually every mark we possess is in this house. Otherwise, since the market crash, our investments have lost their value. Some have turned negative. We have nothing beyond these four walls. And my law practice is not what it was…'

Now the upshot of this information made things more serious. Arno had expected Monika's parents to possess the solution. If a ransom payment was the issue, then their wealth would surely solve it. In a curious way, he'd even once seen them as culprits, living in their expensive district, inviting envy and dissatisfaction from people looking in. But he recognised they were no more in control of the situation than he was.

'We must find out Monika's last movements,' Herr Goldstein began again. 'Who she saw last, who she was in contact with. Clearly, there is more about our daughter we don't know.'

'Do you have any idea where they are keeping her?' Arno asked.

'She is most likely somewhere in the city,' Herr Goldstein replied. 'The criminals are undoubtedly local. That's what we've been advised. Perhaps someone with a prejudice against us. We would not be the first Jewish family to be the subject of something despicable like this. But we will find a way forward. We simply must.'

Herr Goldstein was beginning to locate his lucidity again, and with it, Monika's mother finally entered the room and stood beside her husband.

Arno passed his gaze between the couple. How

exhausted they looked, sagging in their clothes as if they'd both shrunk by a couple of inches. It was then he decided to impart a little information that may give them some hope.

'It may surprise you to know that I have contacts in the police. These aren't the *Kriminalpolizei*, you understand. I can talk to them discreetly. I may be able to find out something useful. I can't promise anything, but I can try.'

Herr Goldstein's first response was, 'No, certainly not, you mustn't speak to the police. It will put our daughter in danger. I forbid it.'

'Listen, I'm not referring to the regular force. There are people who operate covertly so to speak. I can ask subtly.'

'Who do you know? What are you mixed up in?'

'It's impossible for me to say. You have to trust me.'

'You're a student. At the beginning of adulthood. Who on earth could you know?'

'I'm better connected than you think.'

'Are you sure?' Monika's mother asked.

'Whoever has taken Monika, someone will know about it.' He remembered the words of the police agent when they first told him about Vendetta. 'Criminals like this want to extend their territories. They operate underground networks to raise funds and win the support of the lesser men.'

'Win the support of the lesser men? Now you sound like a revolutionary!'

'You're missing the point. Don't you see? This is where we can gain a foothold.'

Monika's parents listened closely. Arno felt his influence in the room rising. With every grain of truth he spoke, he seemed to bring light into the gloomy quarters. Then it occurred to him, that if he was going to succeed he would have to act fearlessly. And to do that, he had to be the risk-taking and foolhardy individual he knew himself to be.

30

At exactly midday, an aubergine-coloured car pulled up in front of Lassner's gallery. Arno got in and slid himself along the leather backseat next to an armed Stormtrooper. In the front were the driver and another soldier, who nodded at him to drive on. As for Göring, he was nowhere in sight.

The car drove to the edge of the city, over several bridges, beyond Tempelhof Airport and the gasworks that marked the industrial edges of Berlin. Arno wound the window down and lit up a cigarette, which lasted little more than thirty seconds in the fierce breeze. The car sped on, taking him deeper into the Party ranks. His penetration into the Nazi world had begun. And his alibi – an art dealer no less! – was his ticket inside.

Eventually, they stopped outside a flat-roofed building along a nondescript suburban road. The Brownshirts, who had held steadfast to a solemn sort of silence, got to their feet and accompanied Arno out of the car. He looked around, up and down the street. There was a tram line at one end and a row of empty-looking houses at the other. Ahead of him, a brick edifice with blacked-out windows reared up like an old bookcase. After the plush quarters of the art gallery, this rundown street seemed little more than a backwater.

Another stern-looking Stormtrooper stood guard at

the door. He had his hand on a brass door handle the shape of a lion's head. As Arno approached, the door was opened and a second Brownshirt came to escort him inside. The young soldier was barely older than a schoolboy and had the keen look of a new recruit.

They went through a hallway with ceramic tiles and up a narrow staircase. 'What is this place?' Arno asked, feeling the adolescent would be less guarded.

'It's one of our warehouses.'

'Warehouse for what?'

'We keep all sorts here. We have the best cigarettes in Germany. Did you know the Party has its own brand?'

The boy took out a packet of cigarettes from his shirt pocket and showed it to Arno. The box was yellow with blue writing. *Trommler Gold* stood out in bold lettering.

'I've seen these around,' Arno said. 'Never smoked one though.'

'Here, have a packet. I've got plenty.' The boy dug around in his oversized trousers that flared up from his black boots. He handed Arno a packet as they went deeper into the maze.

'Anything else here?'

'Nothing else that I'm permitted to know,' the boy said, grinning. 'Only honourable intentions.'

They walked along a corridor that had a rug running the entire length. All of the doors along the corridor were closed and there were no windows; the air was stagnant. As the lad seemed happy to talk, Arno was tempted to ask about Vendetta. Had he heard of it? Was the building they were inside connected? But he decided not to jump in too soon. He suspected Vendetta was a conversation to be had with the higher ranks of the Party.

'I'm taking you to see Oberführer von Hessen,' the boy said, switching to a serious tone. 'He's along here.'

'Hessen?' Arno questioned, recognising the name.

The soldier stopped and glared. 'You sound surprised?' His face was suddenly tight with alarm, like he'd just been slapped.

'I'm here to see Oberführer von Hessen, of course,' Arno corrected. 'I was invited by Göring, I don't know what to expect. I'm an art dealer, not a politician.'

The soldier relaxed. 'Expect the unexpected, that's all I'll say.'

They entered through a pointed archway into a sort of antechamber with a large desk at one end that had a framed picture of Hitler on it. And there, sat at the desk, was the very same man Arno recognised from Café Bauer and Lassner's gallery. He had short blond hair and a lean, healthy-looking face. A small scar at the top of his forehead caught the light and looked like a dent in his skull. He stood up sharply and then walked around his desk in a slow, purposeful rhythm. Arno felt a dark foreboding to finally meet the man.

'Pleased to make your acquaintance,' Arno said.

'So you're the art dealer that Herr Göring professes an admiration for?' Hessen said loudly, shaking Arno's hand. It wasn't obvious if he recognised him from their glances at Lassner's gallery. 'I understand you like to liquidate the assets of corrupt Jewish families?'

Arno bluffed in his reply. 'When an opportunity comes my way, I like to take it.'

'I do the same! You must let me know if you come across any human assets – those I collect!'

'I'm not sure I understand.'

'Antiques and paintings, they're all well and good, but there's nothing like the gamble of a real human being to raise the stakes. The wager for a life can be high, the winnings even higher.' Hessen spoke with flawless arrogance.

Arno found himself clenching his jaw.

There was silence for a moment as Hessen waited expectantly for a response. 'That's why Göring sent you to me, is it not?' the Nazi said. 'To tell me about your Jewish collectibles, to see if you can help me and I, in return, can help you?'

Arno was about to reply when a woman came in carrying a brass tray. On the tray were two glass tumblers and an egg salad on a white plate. She said nothing as she crossed the room slowly. Hessen watched her as she set the tray down on a side table. Then all of a sudden he bounded over in front of her and started howling like a dog. She flinched at his strange antics, raised her arm over her face and left the room in a hurry.

'Her left eye,' Hessen said grinning – 'did you notice, is completely blind? Utterly useless. I keep expecting her to walk into the furniture. One day she will oblige me and I will take great pleasure in dismissing her.' He smiled to himself. 'On second thoughts,' – he turned to the young soldier who was still in attendance – 'have her replaced. Immediately. Find someone younger and prettier. I've had enough of looking at that wrinkled old crone.'

The soldier looked on, uncertain and afraid. 'I have no authority, sir.'

'What?' Hessen asked lightly. 'Do I ask too much of you?'

The soldier stuttered. 'No, I just – I don't.'

'Get rid of her.'

The soldier was mute.

Hessen turned to Arno, still smiling. Then he went over to the soldier, took out his pistol and struck the boy across the face with the blunt end. The soldier crumbled to the floor, holding onto his face as a ribbon of blood ran down his hand and spiralled around his wrist.

Arno watched. His first instinct was to help the lad but he knew he had to hold back. He tried to smile, to pretend he endorsed the violence. Yet the sight of the boy unable to get to his feet, taking rapid gasps of air through his mouth – because his nose was probably broken – held Arno motionless in disgust. Hessen spent a moment hovering over his victim like a prize-fighter over his knockout, then turned to his desk to lay his pistol on it.

'I'm sorry about that. I'm just trying to impress you. I do that sometimes. It's a weakness.'

Arno looked on and swallowed.

'I like to play little games with myself,' Hessen continued. 'Here.' He reached into his trouser pocket. 'Take a look at what I picked up.' He opened his hand and showed Arno a gold tooth. It sat in the centre of his palm like a tiny golden temple. 'It's a Soviet tooth. Extracted from Moscow. A Communist gave it to me. I remember, he smelled foul. I think he'd shit himself. But he did give me this tooth, after a little persuasion. What do you think?'

Hessen held the glistening tooth under Arno's nose.

'Remarkable what you can get your hands on when you're determined,' Hessen said. Then, going to a leather briefcase propped up on a chair, he took out an envelope. Arno noticed it had a name and address already written on it – although it was too far away to read. Hessen slipped the tooth inside the envelope and sealed it shut.

'I'm posting it to myself,' he said. 'Another game I like to play. I have all these envelopes addressed to myself.' He took out a batch of about a dozen envelopes from his case, all of them prepared and stamped. 'If I find something I like the look of, something I imagine I'd like to receive as a gift, I send it to myself. You know,

I have a terribly poor memory, so by the time this gets to me, I will have utterly forgotten that I sent it. It'll be a nice surprise, don't you think?' His eyes took on a rapturous glow. 'A man like you will understand the pleasure of collecting, of course.'

By now, the young Brownshirt was back on his feet. A great spray of blood was drying across his cheek and over the corner of his shoulder.

'Actually, I was hoping to speak to someone such as yourself about a topic I'm particularly interested in.'

'Oh, and what would that be?'

'As I mentioned to Göring, my field is the movement of valuable artworks. But I've also been known to transport contraband when the occasion requires it.'

'Really? How interesting.'

'There are specific road and rail networks I know that make my methods of art dealership virtually invisible.' Arno could see he had Hessen's full attention. 'I can envisage that we could be strong associates – especially when it comes to… Vendetta.'

Hessen was surprised. 'Vendetta? Göring never said he told you about Vendetta? And now you wander in here with that word on your lips.' Hessen then nodded sideways to the young Brownshirt, who disappeared into the corridor.

Arno caught the signal and knew it meant trouble. 'Let me explain.'

At that moment, a consort of six Stormtroopers entered the room. They grabbed Arno under each arm and forced him to his knees. Hessen stood back and watched, mighty and proud.

'Listen to me,' Arno went on, with his arms clutched in a painful brace. 'My allegiance is only to the Party. Recently, I assisted the transport of hundreds of passports. It was just six days ago. The assignment was travelling overnight on the north-west line back to Berlin.'

Hessen listened for a moment. 'Let him go.' He walked up to Arno, who was now back on his feet and dusted his jacket down. 'Leave us. All of you,' he said, waving the Stormtroopers away. 'Apologies, but we have to be vigilant when it comes to Vendetta. It is a strong idea. If it brings the change we want then I'm in favour. We have to be careful, of course, about who gets told what.'

'I have been briefed,' Arno said, clawing his way back in. 'Though I wish to consolidate my position in the Party and join the project at a higher level.'

'Become allies you mean?'

'They were precisely my thoughts.' As he spoke, behind him he heard the door open and footsteps come into the room.

'Ah, now, here is a man who is a greater advocate of Vendetta than any of us.'

Hessen raised his arm to welcome a new visitor into the room. Arno turned, and in through the archway walked none other than Erich Ostwald.

31

'Vendetta!' Erich Ostwald proclaimed loudly as he walked into the room.

Arno was astounded. Yes, he was the same confident, capricious man he remembered. Loose in stride, upbeat, a touch grandiose, even when the occasion didn't call for it.

Erich and Hessen gave the *Sieg Heil!* salute to one another.

'I don't believe it,' Erich said as he turned to Arno. 'Am I really looking at the same Arno Hiller? What a transformation!'

Despite the merry sarcasm, Arno was apprehensive. He had to maintain his cover in Erich's presence. The last time they'd seen each other was nearly three years before when Arno was a skittish youth. The idea that he had become some sort of art expert in Erich's eyes could seem far-fetched. Still, his only choice was to push ahead – especially with the combustible Hessen looking on.

'What a pleasant surprise to see you Erich,' Arno said taking the lead. He passed a glance at Erich with what he affected as certainty in his eyes.

Erich smiled back. He looked like he'd put on weight. His face was plump and ripe like a peach.

'This young man,' Erich said, explaining to Hessen, 'is extremely courageous. We worked together once, do you remember?'

'Of course. In a way, it led me here,' Arno replied.

'We had a scheme to get the Communists into strife, didn't we?' Erich went on, glowing. 'We were both younger then, more inexperienced undoubtedly.' He patted Arno's back.

'Well, a lot has changed since we last met years ago. I'm here on business. Count von Hessen and I were talking about art. I'm now a collector and trader.'

'I'm told he's doing a fine job stripping assets from our Semitic friends,' Hessen interrupted.

'Art?' Erich remarked, his expression perplexed.

'I'm currently connected to the Mattias Lassner gallery,' Arno said, holding his nerve. 'I've achieved much success by visiting the estates of troubled Jewish families on the move. I've just returned from Austria with a very favourable Caravaggio.'

'Yes, Göring was itching to buy that painting but I hear his adviser talked him out of it.'

'Why?'

'His ego probably. He doesn't like the idea of anyone but himself telling Göring what to buy, especially when it comes to collectible items like art.'

Erich went over to the plate of egg salad and forked a yellow yolk into his mouth. 'Caravaggio is a touch melodramatic for me,' he said after swallowing. 'Of the Italians, I lean towards Bellini. I will occasionally tolerate Veronese. Titian is glorious of course, but something about all those heavy allegories puts me off.'

Arno nodded casually in agreement. He was more distracted by what Hessen had said. The news of Göring's adviser being intimidated by Arno seemed a revelation. Maybe his monocled friend wasn't all he was cracked up to be.

'As long as we have your support here, then I'm

pleased,' Erich said, apparently satisfied with Arno's pretence.

'I'd say churning out anti-communist propaganda and supporting Vendetta align rather well,' Arno said, testing his luck. 'Wouldn't you agree?'

'Yes, it would seem so.'

'What's the latest? And how exactly do you fit into the project?'

Arno stared at Erich directly. Of all the ice he'd been skating on, this was the thinnest.

'You expect to be included in discussions do you?' Erich said. His sarcasm seemed to have vanished.

Arno glanced to Hessen, then back to Erich. 'Well, if it's useful for me in serving the Party.'

'Vendetta can wait! I want to hear all about what you've been doing.' There was an air of recklessness in Erich's voice. On the surface, he seemed genuinely pleased to see Arno, but still, there was something fickle in the way he spoke. Part of Arno wanted to abscond from the room before he was found out. The greater part insisted he stay and make the most of this chance meeting. It could be the best opportunity he would get.

He was about to impart a series of fictional stories about travels to various European cities, when Hessen intervened.

'There's no time for small-talk. We have work to be getting on with.' Then turning to Arno. 'A Bavarian dancing band are coming this evening. Please stay with us. We have rooms to spare.'

'Yes!' Erich said briskly. 'You can sleep upstairs and get over your hangover.'

'I don't get hangovers.' Arno responded with a wisecrack.

'You will tomorrow. I guarantee it.'

Arno agreed to stay on, thinking it was a propitious

sign to be invited to stay. For the rest of the afternoon, he was given a table to work at, where he would claim to write notes on his accounts.

At various times he found himself alone.

On the first occasion, he remained rooted to his desk, aware that a window to explore had suddenly presented itself – one that quickly slipped through his fingers. When the second occasion came he got to his feet and made a direct line for Hessen's desk on the other side of the room. He remained cool, knowing the importance of keeping to the attitude of someone who was permitted to be there. He searched the surface of the desk, sifting through papers whilst keeping a lookout for anyone coming.

There were various administrative documents arranged into piles, some with account ledger listings and others with manoeuvres for SA troops. Then, underneath the black telephone, he found a letter of a more personal kind, evidently a plea on behalf of Hessen to borrow money:

'Dear Gustave,

I would not ask if conditions had not forced me to. Be sure that I know quite well how many people depend on you and that requests of this kind come to you daily. But I have a duty to ask: an amount of 3,000 marks would be more than sufficient to cover my most pressing debts.

Efforts remain occupied with establishing Vendetta. Once the project is sufficiently entrenched, I will be able to place my attention back on our friendship, which I know you remain impatient to return to.

Yours,
Hermann'

Arno moved on from the letter. Hessen's financial

circumstances were interesting given his lavishness but it wasn't the concrete evidence of Vendetta he was looking for. He pulled on several of the desk drawers but all were locked shut.

Next, he went to a glass-fronted bookcase that stood behind. He opened one of the doors to find routine procedural files and different service contracts. There was no hint of Vendetta. The trail was cold. He went back to Hessen's desk, cursing to himself. But then he knew he had to be more shrewd. He slowly looked across the desk once more, scanning every item.

Then he noticed something right in front of him. It was a racehorse statue on the right-hand side with a figure mounted on top. But instead of holding a riding crop, the figure held a small slender key. It was so subtle, you could easily miss it. Arno carefully slid the key out, wondering where it would fit, until he saw that the desk itself was antique and primed for such a delicate object.

He put the key into one of the locked drawers, finding it turned three-hundred-and-sixty degrees that ended with a click. Opening the drawer quietly, he pulled out a book with the *Reichsadler* eagle crest embossed on the front. Inside was a collection of bound documents. He lifted it onto the desk and cascaded through the pages. Most of the contents referenced the movement of Brownshirts – he saw mention of a parade planned for Unter den Linden avenue; in another, proposals for a demonstration at Fasanen Strasse Synagogue near the Kurtürstendamm.

Then, finally, he found something more solid. It was a document that listed the movement of weapons using the rail network from outside of Berlin into the city. It had to be related to Vendetta, just like the passport smuggling when he first met Hannah Baumer. He was tempted to tear out the page and take it away with him from the warehouse. Anything he could lay his hands on that might satisfy the police was useful. They were almost certainly anticipating information from him soon.

Just then, the telephone began to ring. He looked down again at the paperwork – would someone miss it if he took it? The ringing continued, at which he quickly closed the book and slid it back into the drawer. Then there was the sound of a door opening down the corridor. Someone was coming.

Footsteps from along the hallway grew louder. He hooked the key back on the statue before traversing the room back to his own desk. A moment later, an SA soldier entered and answered the telephone. 'He is not here,' the conversation began. Arno listened in earnest. 'What is the name?' the Brownshirt said, at which he seemed to become conscious of Arno in the room and turned his back. The conversation ended with the name 'Poelzig.'

The Brownshirt hung up the telephone and looked across at Arno. He then noticed the glass door of the bookcase behind was ajar. Without a word, he pushed it closed, then began stalking the room with an aggrieved air, like a trapped fly unwilling to settle.

'Oberführer von Hessen left just twenty minutes ago,' Arno offered, trying to guess at the Nazi's purpose.

'I'll speak to him later, in that case,' came the reply. The man had a craggy face and a ginger crop of hair. His lip curled with hostility when he came over and looked over Arno's desk. 'You look busy,' he said, his tone teetering on contempt.

'Indeed I am,' Arno asserted back, as the Brownshirt brusquely left the room.

32

That evening the same Nazi kept his eyes pinned on Arno. Every time Arno looked up, the man's glare was already on him. What did he suspect? Moreover, what was he going to do about it?

From eight o'clock on, the Bavarian evening unfolded. There were great platters of food at first, followed by several rounds of drinking games. Then, when everyone was suitably dazed, a dancing show began.

Arno pretended to enjoy himself, as if he could prove his credentials by blending in with the merriment. His performance was forced but it must have been convincing, as the staring eyes of the Brownshirt eventually unhooked themselves from him and drifted elsewhere.

What he really wanted to do was slip away but the place was swarming with Brownshirts. Even so, he kept an eye on the main entrance; when it was clear, he took his chance and ventured into the corridor. Hessen's office would be empty now.

Yet within seconds, he was interceded by two armed soldiers. He said he was looking for the restroom, at which they signalled him in the opposite direction, forcing Arno to turn back towards the party.

On his return, he happened to notice some activity in

one of the cloakrooms. There was a man hovering in the shadows. Arno stopped. He took care not to be seen as he watched the stranger. The man, who wasn't a soldier, was consumed by his task, which consisted of riffling through the pockets of all the coats on the rack.

Garment by garment he went, dipping his hand into every pouch and crevice. At first, Arno took him to be a thief, but there was something unusually methodical about the way he was hunting through the coats. He was extremely deliberate; every so often he stopped and made a note of something he'd seen, using a small black book and a pen had he propped behind his ear.

A moment or two later, a kitchen hand came rattling down the corridor, pushing a trolley of plates and cutlery. The man was disturbed and looked up, at which Arno retreated to make himself scarce. When he passed the cloakroom again, the strange figure had disappeared.

Arno returned to the party where the Bavarian dancing troupe was in full swing. There were five dancers in all, three men and two women. To the rhythm of an accordion player, they made over-the-top gestures, leaping and pinching each other's backsides, grabbing each other by the shoulders and slapping one another's feet. It was all very absurd. The men lifted the women's skirts and in return the women giggled coyly. By the end, two couples had paired off, leaving one man as the lonely stooge to be laughed at or sympathised with, depending on your disposition. Everyone seemed to have enjoyed it immensely, but to Arno it was old-fashioned and ridiculous; above all, he was far too distracted to care.

A short time later he felt a tapping on his shoulder. It was Erich, summoning Arno to join himself and Hessen at their table. Arno sat down and unfolded his napkin. When he looked up, he came face to face with the stranger he'd seen in the cloakroom fifteen minutes earlier. The same plunderer who'd taken an avid interest in the contents of other people's jackets was sat directly opposite him. What was more curious was his self-assured bearing, and the way he glanced around the table with a wily unshaven face.

Hessen noticed Arno looking. 'Perhaps you'd like me to introduce you? This gentleman is Ringel. He is a magician of the first order. And a dear friend of mine.'

At this point, a woman from along the table spoke up. 'You must be the famous clairvoyant.'

Ringel dipped his head modestly.

'I would very much like to see you perform. Why don't you show us one of your tricks.'

Hessen stepped in. 'This isn't the right time.'

But the woman insisted. 'Please. Let him show us what he can do. I'm sure we'd all like to see.'

Ringel raised his head and locked eyes with the woman. He seemed to assess her for a moment before agreeing to her demands.

'Come, I'll be your guinea pig,' she said.

'I would insist on it,' Ringel replied in a steady voice.

'What would you like me to do?'

'Silence your mind, shut out all distractions and focus only on me.'

'Very well.'

Ringel gazed along the tabletop towards the woman and held her stare. 'I see you are a lady of wide horizons,' he said. 'Even whilst at this gathering, half of your mind is elsewhere. You are travelling soon. Am I right?'

'I will confirm nothing,' she said, smirking.

'You expect to take a journey. I see mountains and lakes. But that is not your destination. That is merely the journey, over the Alps perhaps. South. I see the letter, P. Pisa? No, that's not it. Palermo? No that's not the place either. I see somewhere very old, a lost city.' Ringel then closed his eyes for a minute before he reopened them to confirm his prediction, 'Pompeii! You are travelling to Naples and you expect to visit the ancient ruins.'

All eyes now turned to the woman.

'Well, that is remarkable! I am due to travel tomorrow. I have a train ticket here in my handbag. I can prove it.' She opened up her handbag and began to search inside. 'It's here somewhere. That's very impressive. How did you know?'

A round of applause now erupted around the table and everyone's attention turned to Ringel. 'Bravo!' Erich shouted. Unsurprisingly to Arno, the woman was left hunting through her handbag.

'Why don't you do me next?' Arno said, volunteering himself.

Ringel looked dubiously at Arno, as he pressed his hands together and slid his fingers together.

'I'm finished now,' he said, smiling at Hessen.

'Oh and why is that?' Arno pressed.

'Herr Hiller, let the man stop if he wishes,' Hessen said a little tersely.

'Of course,' Arno said. 'The powers of divination are fickle.'

Ringel raised his eyebrows.

Hessen gave a troubled smile. 'Sir, you cannot insult the genius of Ringel. He is a true magician and clairvoyant. He sells out at theatres because he has the gift. He has had the gift since childhood.'

Ringel then reached out his arm to Arno. 'Give me your hand.'

Arno lent forward with his open palm, which Ringel grasped and started to inspect.

'Interesting. You are troubled. You have lost something precious to you.'

Arno looked on tight-lipped. 'What is it?'

'Something very important to you.'

'Yes.' An image of Monika came to him, thoughts he pushed away.

'Something you cannot live without!'

Arno and Ringel looked soberly at one another. The other companions around the table waited in anticipation.

'Tell me.'

Ringel released Arno's palm and clasped his hands together. 'Your sense of humour!'

Everyone around the table burst into laughter. Hessen started howling, tears streaming down his cheeks. Erich slapped Arno on the back in jest.

Arno feigned a smile, now that the tension had eased. 'You nearly had me going there,' he said, holding his heart.

He knew Ringel had nothing on him. What was more interesting was Hessen's reaction: he was clearly beholden to Ringel and protective too.

The magician bowed his head as the feast and drinks were brought over and spread across the table. Everyone had their fill, although when the wine was served Ringel placed his hand over the glass in front of him. Then Arno noticed that when each course was placed before Ringel he waved the food away, seemingly unable to stomach anything.

'You're not eating?' Arno pointed out.

'I have no appetite.'

'Are you unwell?'

'Do I look unwell?' Ringel snapped.

Everyone around the table fell silent.

'My apologies,' Arno said. 'I didn't mean to cause offence.'

'None taken,' Ringel said, rising from his seat. 'It's

time I left.'

'Come on people, this is supposed to be a party,' Erich exclaimed as Ringel sloped off.

'Yes it is. We need to amuse ourselves,' Hessen said, signalling to one of the Brownshirts with a glance.

The ginger-haired soldier rose from the table and abruptly left the room. He returned minutes later with a new addition to the party. It was a girl. She was not part of the dancing troupe and was a far more reluctant accessory to the entertainment. The Brownshirt dragged her by the hand into the middle of the room, whereby a great wave of raucous laughter rose to the ceiling. The girl was trying to resist, pulling away from the soldier, who jerked her back into place. When she stood still, Arno could see her hands were shaking. Her hair had fallen forward over her bowed head. The Brownshirt – a fat man with cherry-red cheeks – attempted some ham-fisted delicacy as he drew back her hair and tried to dance with her.

At this point, Arno felt his heart almost explode. With alarm, he sat up in his seat, not wanting to believe his eyes. It was her. It was Monika. He'd never felt so sick with dejection and horror. He wanted to tear over and prise them apart, punching and kicking the Brownshirt in his oversized head.

An agonising throb went through him as he knew he had to resist. Make the wrong move now and it could be all over for him and Monika. Then it struck him. The name he heard the Brownshirt disclose in Hessen's office – 'Poelzig.' That was the name of the man who sent him the note at the hotel saying he'd found his wallet.

He sat back in his chair and painfully watched on, with a torrent of nerves, anger and shame running through him. Monika was doing her best to pull away from the Brownshirt, whilst also seeming to know that if she struggled too much she was liable to end up in a worse situation. Her posture stiffened and she turned her head sideways, looking away from the Brownshirt and back to the door she'd just come through. She was still wearing her nightgown; a bed blanket wrapped over her shoulders had fallen to the floor. She hadn't spotted Arno yet, but any moment now, she would.

ENDINGS

33

The man who stood in Monika's doorway had the bulky silhouette of a bear. Half-drunk, he lumbered inside and hauled her from her bed by the arm. She managed to grab a blanket and lift it over her shoulders as she was led along the nocturnal corridors by the meatloaf of a man.

Pushed through a doorway, she found herself in a room of complete disorder, where a fog of beer and cigarette smoke loomed over a hoard of drunken soldiers. She was forced to dance in humiliation with the fat Brownshirt, who kept taking thirsty gulps from a glass of beer as he held onto her. But the thing that Monika became truly aware of in that awful room was the face of Arno Hiller.

Her first instinct was to call out to him. For a moment she felt a glint of hope to see his bright face. She'd suffered alone for nearly a week. To finally lay her eyes on someone familiar was an earth-shattering relief. Yet her deliverance quickly collapsed as she began to comprehend where she was. The raucous party boomed and rocked around her, a sweaty stinking room full of ungodly men revelling in the eerie music.

In that instant, she realised that everything the police had told her about Arno was completely true. His involvement with this herd of beasts was impossible to doubt now. He was there, in plain sight among them.

She didn't want to look at him but her eyes were irresistibly drawn. His face seemed to bob in the air with his recognisable features just hanging there, white and exposed, floating in complete silence.

She felt entirely removed from her body as the Brownshirt lifted her arms into a waltzing posture and pushed his belly into her. They danced slowly and clumsily in circles as an accordion rolled out its rhythm. The fat man was inept and kept trying to hoist her closer, but she remained floppy and listless like a rag-doll. It seemed as if they were both puppets of a joke, engaged in this embrace with a room full of monsters grinning at them and stamping in time to the music. At a certain point, they all stood and sang some old marching song, *Never Say Die*, which was an ugly din and fell into disarray soon into the second verse.

Only Arno remained impassive. He never moved a muscle, never smiled nor opened his mouth to sing. He only looked expressionless, occasionally lowering his eyes to the floor.

After ten minutes of this ridicule, her turn was over. General Hessen stepped in and said something about 'Keeping this one for himself' – a phrase that sent shivers through her. She raced back to her room and shut the door. After that, the night was long and dismal. She wondered if Arno would come to her. She wanted him to come but was also afraid of what would happen if he did. Would he find her and expect to gain entrance to her room? Would he be the same Arno she once fell in love with, or would he show his true colours as the new monstrosity she had discovered?

She lay in her bed for several hours and couldn't sleep. She hated feeling afraid, and with this thought, she slowly brought herself round to the point where her fear began to drop away. Arno was no more than a stranger to her now. The more she accepted this, the more her despondency lifted. She was trapped and resigned herself to it once and for all.

As the party wore on, Arno began to understand that the men he was with were little more than a gang of savages. The reality dawned on him earlier in the night when one of the Brownshirts began bragging about how, only the day before, he'd picked up the wife of a Communist protester and sliced her mouth open with a broken bottle. The Nazi made a gesture with his fingers, pulling his own smile to twice its width to indicate the effect. The rest of the men, some fifteen of them – including Hessen and Erich – sat back in their seats and warmed themselves over the story as if beside a cosy fireplace.

What Arno found strange was how their manners remained civil – raucous yes, but strangely courteous too. It was like a game of cards: when each man's turn came, he laid down his hand with a casual, poker-faced amiability. Even in the throes of debauchery, appearances still mattered.

After the story of the Communist's wife, there followed a round of one-upmanship. Another soldier said he had recently punched a man so hard that his two front teeth had lodged into his knuckles. He offered a dashed scar-line on his fist to prove it. The man next to him said he'd once worked as a border guard and bribed a Jew by confiscating his passport and not returning it until he had handed over ten-thousand marks.

'The Jewess upstairs,' someone asked Hessen, 'how much do you expect to get for her?'

Hessen replied with the assured tone of an accountant that he expected to gain up to fifty-thousand marks for the transaction. Now that Monika had been paraded in front of them, Arno knew that he was spending the night with her kidnappers. Drinking and smoking with them, forced into being jovial alongside them. That was the cost of becoming an informant, or more importantly to get Monika out of their clutches.

The party lasted till five in the morning. Arno was desperate to get away but waited until everyone fizzled out and went to bed. To think that Monika was in the very same building as he was made him rage with agony. He decided two things during the course of that wretched party: the first was that he detested the National Socialists and all they stood for with all his being; the second was that he would be prepared to die at their hands if it meant he could set Monika free.

As the first faint rays of sun began to rise, a cockerel crowed. The party was over and Arno pretended to turn in. His head throbbed with the grim residue of the night before and his clothes reeked with the stale reminders of everything he had consumed. Eventually, the building around him fell into silence.

He then went from his room out into the corridor where the walls glowed golden with the approaching morning. There was nothing to suggest which wing Monika was being kept in and with no bearings inside the building he had little clue where to begin.

As he scoured the corridors, he was able to make his way back to the hall where the Bavarian party had taken place and then through the entrance where they'd brought Monika in. Ahead of him ran a long corridor lined with doors on both sides. If he tried the handle of every single one, sooner or later he might find her, but there was more chance of waking a tired out Nazi and getting pistol-whipped with that strategy.

He went along the corridor, trying not to stir a

sound. Every time he put his foot down, the floorboard he was treading on or else the board he was lifting from gave a low whining sound. He imagined the brown-shirted men asleep behind each of the doors, deeply submerged in their drunken dreams, snoring, snuffling and turning over in their bedsheets as the floorboards half-woke them.

He began to think he was the only one in the building to be awake, which gave him an advantage. The simple question was: where were they keeping Monika? At the end of the corridor, he came to a stairway that he climbed.

At the top, he came to a small landing narrowly squeezed with two doors. One was a cupboard with a boiler inside. The other was a pantry with an enormous chest of drawers, several industrial-sized bags of flour and about twenty trays of eggs stacked into piles. A lancet-shaped window gave a view over an inner courtyard, above which the sky was milky-blue with light.

It was a dead end, and with only the descending staircase to return down, he suddenly realised he was not alone. The same moaning floorboards he had walked a few moments before were making the same groans. Then he heard footsteps coming up the stairs towards him.

He looked down to find it was the old maid coming towards him. She was carrying a stack of plates cleaned up from the party. She didn't look up but remained absorbed in transporting her ceramic cargo. He crept into the pantry and hid behind the door. And as soon as she came in and put the plates down, Arno put his hand over her mouth. He assured her that he wouldn't harm her if she didn't draw any attention.

'I need to know which room the girl is in,' he whispered.

The woman looked at him, her eyes never once blinking. He saw that her blindness was confined to just one eye, which was clouded and warped like a glass marble.

'There is a Jewish girl being kept here. Do you know who I mean?'

The woman nodded, to which he uncupped her mouth.

'You don't need to bother with her. I don't see why it's any of your business.'

Arno became aware he'd been too strong in his first approach. He let his body relax, slouched a little and gave a smile. 'I'm just someone who likes a pretty girl,' he said, trying to sound indifferent, playing the cad. 'Now, why don't you tell me which room she is in so I can pay her a compliment.'

The woman shook her head.

'It's very important that I speak to her,' Arno said.

The woman said nothing.

'What's the matter with you?' he said. 'Don't you understand you're supposed to do as you're told? Don't you know I'm more important than you?'

The woman turned to face him. 'Be serious,' she said. 'You're not one of them. I can tell by the way you look and speak. It's not their way. Why are you sneaking about up here?'

Arno felt like he wanted to strangle the old woman but came up with a different idea.

'Perhaps you could give her a message. If I write something, would you give it to her?'

'Maybe,' she said. 'That girl is not to be toyed with, mind you. Do you understand?'

'I would never do that,' Arno said. 'Never.'

As the woman tidied around the pantry, he found a scrap of paper and hurriedly wrote out a note. It was a cryptic attempt at reassurance, written in the guise of a romantic admission.

'Dear girl,

Have we met before? In a dream perhaps? If the rest of them teased you, I wanted to protect you. Please realise, that I cannot express myself fully in just a few words. Only to say, art and life meet in your aspect.

Yours,
An admirer'

He folded the note and gave the slip of paper to the maid. He knew perfectly well that it would be read, certainly by the old lady and possibly by the Nazis too. He hoped they would just tease him for it; and if they did, that meant his coded words had gone undetected.

34

Later that morning, Arno accepted the offer of a car back to the centre of Berlin. He went immediately to a telephone booth at the Adlon Hotel and rang the Goldstein household. A housemaid took a message: that they should meet him at Café Vits on Grunewald Strasse at two o'clock that afternoon.

Arno made his way across Pariser Platz and south down to Kaiserhof U-Bahn station. He travelled three stops on the underground before changing trains at Nollendorfplatz, before a couple more stops to Bayerischer Platz. He stepped out onto Grunewald Strasse and walked the remaining distance to Café Vits. He found a table in view of the entrance and then began to flick through a copy of the *Berliner Morgen-Zeitung* to blend into the surroundings. He smoked half a cigarette but stubbed it out because it was making him jittery. Or rather it was the fact the Nazis had Monika. There was also the name 'Poelzig' playing on his mind: it was uncommon enough but to come across the name again in Hessen's office was hard to ignore.

A waiter approached, politely took an order for a drink and shuffled off with an obedient nod. The Goldsteins were late. His only objective was to convince them not to pay the ransom or do anything that involved the police. He felt sure he could get Monika out of the

Nazi's clutches unscathed and without bankrupting her family. Exactly how would all depend on the Goldsteins.

As he waited, he kept an eye out for any SA brutes or anyone else who might have cause to follow him. He'd thought it was better to meet in public rather than go directly to the Goldstein house, in case it was being monitored. Café Vits, well-known to the locals of Schöneberg district for its gigantic pastry counter, had a series of horseshoe-shaped booths that would give them sufficient privacy.

He retrieved his stubbed-out cigarette from the ashtray and lit it again. At the same moment, he saw Herr and Frau Goldstein arrive through the entrance, dipping their heads beneath the entrance curtain and looking around warily. Their faces carried the grave look of prolonged anguish and their bodies had a stooping gait as if years had passed.

Arno stood up and gave a discreet wave to bring them over. The couple wove slowly through the maze of chairs towards him.

'You have news?' Herr Goldstein asked as he pulled out a chair for his wife to sit on. 'May I ask: how?'

'Yes, my contacts have been very useful.'

'So you have information directly from them?' Herr Goldstein sat down. With a flick of his hand, he sent the waiter away. He was in a more robust state than Arno expected.

'I know where Monika is,' Arno said quickly, getting to the heart of things.

Herr Goldstein remained expressionless. Frau Goldstein bowed her head a little, perhaps afraid of what Arno was going to say next.

'I've discovered she's being kept in a warehouse on the outskirts of the city. It's just as you thought: she was taken by a gang of local criminals.'

Frau Goldstein responded with a low moan of agony.

'Is she okay?' her husband asked.

'She hasn't been seriously harmed. The secret police know where she is, but they are not willing to do anything until they are ready.'

'Ready for what?'

'They are focused on a separate operation going on. It's government business. They can't jeopardise the investigation at such a sensitive stage.'

Herr and Frau Goldstein looked at each other. 'What operation? Why would it have anything to do with Monika?'

Arno felt his throat going dry. He had to be careful about how much he revealed.

'What is our daughter involved with?' Monika's mother pleaded.

He pushed on with an explanation, one that didn't involve himself. 'It is believed that the kidnappers and the political agitators are one and the same. They think Monika was a chance opportunity. The criminals picked her up – somewhere – at random – and now they want to exploit the situation.'

'They've told us where they want the money dropped,' Frau Goldstein said in a hushed tone, glancing at her husband for permission to offer the information.

'You've had another instruction?'

'It was by telephone call yesterday,' Herr Goldstein confirmed.

'Where did they say?'

'In Kreuzberg. Where the elevated S-Bahn line passes over Wiener Strasse.'

'Do you mean at Kottbusser Tor, where the station sits above the road?'

'Yes.' Herr Goldstein began rubbing the back of his

knuckles with this thumb. It was obvious that underneath Monika's father was frantic.

Kottbusser Tor was an overground station raised up on stilts. It was only a short walk from Arno's home at Hallesches. The various roads that met at the intersection passed through the rail arches beneath Kottbusser. He tried to work out why Hessen would want to arrange the drop-off point there, of all places in the city. Then it struck him. They could bring Monika by train from either east or west. And there were at least four roads that led off the junction if they used a motorcar. He remembered there was also a tram line, as well as a forest of iron archways to disappear into. And if they needed more options, the Landwehr Canal was only a stone's throw away. In consideration, it was a perfect location to make an exchange like that. It could happen in an instant, with the perpetrators able to vanish in ten different directions all at once.

'When will it take place?' Arno asked.

Herr Goldstein continued to show reluctance. 'We've said enough. My understanding was that you brought us here because *you* knew something.'

'You're under no obligation to tell me anything,' Arno said. 'But I believe I have a way of getting Monika back. Except, I must know all the details if I'm going to help you.'

'Eight o'clock on Friday evening,' Herr Goldstein said abruptly. 'As the second letter said, they want the money paid in used one-hundred mark notes. It should be delivered by me, alone, in a car going exactly twenty kilometres per hour. I must drive on for half a mile, then turn around and return. Monika will then be released to us.'

'We have arranged to hire a car,' Frau Goldstein said.

'So you intend to pay the money?'

'We'll try. If we beg and borrow, we can raise just over two-thirds of it. It's the best we can do. It will ruin us, but that cannot be worse than seeing our daughter harmed.'

Arno frowned. Hessen was unlikely to accept anything less than the full ransom. He might even interpret it as an insult. 'Whatever you do, don't pay the ransom,' he said forcibly. 'Don't pay a single mark. Even if Monika is returned, which you cannot be sure of, you will have nothing left afterwards. Don't pay it. I have an alternative way that will cost you nothing.'

'We cannot endanger Monika any further,' Herr Goldstein said, interlinking his fingers. 'I fear your promises are meaningless. Why should we believe you? You've really told us nothing today, and in return, we have given you everything we have. It's time for us to be leaving now. Please, young man, do not contact us again.'

Herr Goldstein looked at his wife, and between them, they seemed to come to an agreement.

Arno realised he had to offer something concrete and meaningful to keep them in their seats.

'I have an object in my possession that covers what has been asked in the ransom. I would be willing to offer it as the payment. The kidnappers can do what they want with it – sell it, auction it – whatever they choose.'

'What object?'

'A painting. A very rare and valuable painting. It is mine to do with as I wish.'

'A painting? Why would you do that?'

'Because to me the object is meaningless. Whereas Monika's life is more important. I can put it to good use.'

'No. The kidnappers asked for money. They asked specifically for cash. Why would they accept a painting? It makes no sense.'

'Because the painting is worth double the ransom. That should be reason enough.'

'Where, may I ask, did you lay your hands on a rare painting?'

'I have – well – found some success as an art dealer. My uncle was a collector and introduced me to the field. This precious object has come to me without a financial outlay on my part. That is the benefit of having family connections and a little expertise.'

'An art dealer?' Herr Goldstein seemed barely convinced. 'I thought you were studying?'

'Quite so. Although I have changed subjects. I am now studying the history of art in order to aid my collecting.'

'No,' Herr Goldstein said. 'It's not credible.'

'The painting has a history of ownership which can be traced.' Arno recited the script about the painting's provenance, listing the roll call of names, Cardinal di Ripetta, Guido Reni from the Bolognese School, Francesco Savelli and the Brigandi family. 'Then recently the painting came into my possession.'

The Goldsteins turned to gaze at one another. Arno watched them for what seemed like several minutes – in which the Goldsteins appeared to be reading one another's thoughts.

'We will consider it,' Herr Goldstein eventually said, impressed with Arno's description. 'Today is Wednesday. We have until Friday evening to organise the payment. Where can we reach you?'

'I have no telephone, but I will call you from a public telephone tomorrow morning just after dawn.' Arno extended his palm as Herr Goldstein stood up.

Herr Goldstein looked nervously at Arno, then took his hand and shook it in a firm single motion. 'Come darling,' he spoke to his wife who seemed a little pale. As she rose to put her gloves on she fell limp, stumbling into Herr Goldstein.

'A glass of water quickly,' Arno called out to the waiter as he helped Frau Goldstein back to her seat.

'It's all the stress,' Herr Goldstein said as he bent down on his knees and kissed his wife's hand.

'Maybe. But it's probably the Tisha B'va that's caused it,' she said, steadying herself.

'What's that?' Arno asked.

'It's an annual fast, as a mark of remembrance of our faith.'

A waiter then came over and offered to call a doctor.

'No, I'm okay now,' she said turning the water away. 'Let's go home Felix.'

'Are you sure?'

'Positive.'

Within thirty seconds, Monika's parents had left Café Vits and vanished into the city.

For a while, Arno sat by himself and drank his coffee. In that instant, an idea thrust forward from his mind. Circumstances had convened to bring him to Café Vits but now he was aware of a further possibility from the previous evening's events. Another factor he would look into and soon.

He quickly stepped out from the cool shadows of the café, and then stopped for a moment to think as he looked down along the thoroughfare. A chaotic scene of horse-carts and motorcars, market-stalls and businessmen spread out all the way up the street, all of them oblivious to one another. All of them locked into their own private concerns and obsessions.

He took out his packet of *Trommler Gold* cigarettes and lodged one in his mouth, then strode down the steps to find a hardware store with a post office counter. As soon as he reached one, he went in under the guise of intending to send a telegram. He wrote out a note that contained a specific request, then instead of sending it through the postal service, he folded the paper up and left the store.

Now he had something to hunt for. He recollected the location of the grey postbox that the Prussian Police had stipulated he should submit his findings to. He found the deserted-looking postbox half masked by a curtain of ivy and slipped the note into its mouth. He'd marked it urgent.

He then continued to walk, alive to the weight of his duty – to Monika, to her parents, to himself. He knew that if he could fulfil this assignment and broker the transaction according to the terms he had designed, then Monika should be freed.

Sooner or later he reached the station at Kottbusser Tor and the elevated tracks that crossed the intersection of Skalitzer Strasse and Wiener Strasse. He had made it to the Kreuzberg district of Berlin. It was time to cultivate his next steps.

35

Arno took some time to scout around the station. It was an iron and glass structure that straddled the crossroads like an enormous spider over a web. Between the girders, steps led from the street level up to the station platform. He pictured the direction the Goldstein car might arrive from, slowing to its appropriate speed towards the station and depositing the suitcase of cash. Or if things went to Arno's plan, it wouldn't be cash inside the suitcase, it would be the Caravaggio painting.

He judged that by eight o'clock in the evening the street would be dark. There were lamps along the pavement, but these would give only a dim light and couldn't be counted on to illuminate the finer details of the artwork. He pictured Hessen looking over the object. Where would they be? Lurking beneath the arches? Maybe Erich would be there too? Would they accept the painting instead of the cash? They would be crazy not to, given the amount of money it could yield.

He would insist he was there at the exchange, influencing their decision, weighing things in their favour. He had to convince them just as he'd managed to persuade Göring and his side-kick that the painting was genuine. There was no room for doubt in his mind. It was daring and bold – and these facets seemed to make it more possible still.

The clocks of the city struck two as he came in from the street. Inside his attic, he went straight to the window at the far end and stared over the familiar view as he contemplated the prospective events. A choppy sea of rooftops and gables spread out before him. He drank a beer and then made his way to Käthe and Thomas' apartment two miles away.

'Are you on your own?' he asked when Thomas answered.

'Well yes, Käthe's at her club.'

'Thought she might be,' Arno said, breezing through the front door. 'I need to talk to you.'

'Actually, there's something I wanted to speak to you about,' Thomas said, butting in insistently as he shut the front door. 'Maybe you could shed some light?'

'Let's go through,' Arno replied, as they went into the drawing room.

'I haven't told Käthe because I didn't want to alarm her, but I believe I saw Erich Ostwald a few days ago. Here, in Berlin. I'm sure it was him. What do you think?'

'Where was this?'

'Just on a street corner near Friedrichstrasse. I was shocked because he was wearing a Nazi uniform. Breeches, boots, the swastika emblem – the whole outfit. I thought it couldn't be him, not dressed up like that. I wanted to know, have you heard from him since the letter?'

Given the prior attachments between the three of them, Arno came forward to answer. 'Yes. I met with him – by chance actually.'

'You have? When?'

Arno hesitated. 'If truth be told, it's for the same reason I've come to see you. I'm involved with something serious. It's best I tell *someone*.'

'What is it? What's happened?'

'This is strictly between us. Swear it.'

'Yes, okay,' Thomas said.

Thomas took a chair next to the writing bureau, whilst Arno stood in the middle of the room – centre stage.

'A situation has occurred – I don't know how it happened. Monika too. She's involved.' Arno pushed up his shirt sleeves. 'The first thing was this: Monika and I went away for a few days, just like I told you. We stayed in a hotel. Except, while we were there she vanished. I looked for her everywhere. I thought she must have returned to Berlin so I came back to the city by myself, but on returning I found no sign of her. She wasn't with her parents or with any friends. The next thing I knew, I found myself being propositioned by the police. They wanted me to work for them. They knew all about me and Erich and the anti-Communist activities we instigated years ago. It was the police who told me that Erich was back in Berlin. That's why they wanted to recruit me, because Erich and I have that connection.'

'They recruited you and told you about Erich? I thought you said he wrote you a letter?'

'No, I made that part up. It was easier to say that rather than the truth.'

'What is Erich up to?'

'He's deeply embedded within the National Socialists' Party. I saw him at one of their warehouses. There's a group of them there, running a whole operation. They have offices and accommodation. Erich is involved with something else too, a plot called Vendetta.'

'Vendetta? What's that?'

'It's some sort of insurgence plot. It's what the police expect me to find out about. That's why I was at the warehouse. They think there's a revolution being planned.'

'An uprising?'

'A putsch. A takeover of the government.'

'That's what Erich is planning? I don't believe it.'

'Erich is more involved than anyone.'

'What about Monika? Where is she now?'

'That's the other thing: I saw her too. She's being kept at the warehouse. She was taken. A high-ranking general called Von Hessen is holding her hostage.'

'You mean she's been kidnapped. Do the police know?'

'I'm not sure. It isn't clear-cut. These people claim to be the secret police and its smoke and mirrors with them. Besides, the Nazis have demanded a ransom for her. Her parents want to pay but they can't afford it. I'm going to help them.'

'My God. Have they harmed her?'

'No, not that I can tell. I know her, she's strong. But she'll be scared deep down. I'm certain of that.'

Thomas sat back, trying to take it all in. He loosened his tie and opened his top button. 'You're playing with fire Arno.' He began to think of his old friendship with Erich and how, when the truth of things emerged, he realised there were some things about his friend he knew nothing about. He had come to recognise that Erich was a mystery and there was a great deal he didn't understand back then. He'd supposed that he would never resolve those questions, but now, with Arno's urgent words raining down on him, he recognised that the answers had simply been postponed – until now.

'Monika is all I care about,' Arno went on. 'The police can go to hell and Erich means nothing to me. Monika is the only thing that matters. I don't care if it puts me in danger. I've got to get her out of there.'

'I could pay the ransom. How much is it?'

'No Thomas, it's too much. Anyway, I can cover it. I have a valuable painting that I'm going to offer as the payoff.'

Thomas began scratching his brow. 'I don't understand. A painting?'

'I'm learning to be an art dealer.'

'What?' Thomas laughed. 'An art dealer?' He turned to the window as if some explanation lay in the far distance. 'An art dealer?' he repeated.

'That's right. I'm working in a gallery buying and selling art. The Nazis think I specialise in procuring paintings from Jewish families. That's my cover story.'

Thomas could see Arno was deadly serious, which for him was simply out of character. 'Go on.'

Arno explained about Lassner and the gallery, about the Caravaggio painting and the letters sent to the Goldsteins. As his explanation unfolded, Thomas could see Arno had made his mind up about how he intended to deal with things. What he needed was moral support.

'Tell me what I can do?'

Arno turned aside. 'In case things don't go according to plan and something happens to me, tell Monika and Käthe I wanted them to be safe.'

'It won't come to that surely?'

'Not if I have anything to do with it, but there's no telling how things will go. If the Nazis get the better of me, I want you to do something. Go to my attic room and look above the loft joint that hangs over the window.'

'What will I find?'

'The information I have on Vendetta. There'll also be instructions on what to do with it.'

Thomas was shocked but eventually agreed to the terms.

Arno thanked him and made his way back to

Hallesches Tor. As he hurried through the busy streets, he eventually reached Café Kaiser – the place that bubbled away under his building beyond the twilight hours, when suddenly his path was blocked. It was dark but he recognised the figure as the same man who had delivered his initial work dossier from the police. The man took an envelope from his inside trenchcoat pocket and gave it to Arno.

'We hope this answers your questions,' he said, before stepping aside and moving on.

Arno raced up to his attic room and tore open the envelope. After reading its contents, he sat on the bed and took a deep breath in and out. The news was astounding. Still, he would keep it to himself.

All that mattered was that the exchange went off without a glitch. The only thing he hadn't accounted for was Göring and making sure he wasn't present at the exchange. Göring had already seen the painting and would undoubtedly see the duplicity of the exchange. Somehow, Arno had to ensure he remained absent.

36

Following the torment from the party the night before, Monika woke to find a note had been slipped under her door. She saw it resting on the floorboards – like the palm of a hand stretching towards her.

The pale rays of morning light lay in silent stretches like shadows in reverse across the room. She picked up the note and took it back to bed. It was such a strange letter. At first, it sounded like a chat-up, presumably a prank by one of the soldiers. But there was also a humble quality to it. *'If the rest of them teased you, I wanted to protect you.'* Monika's eyes filled with tears. The line which said *'I cannot express myself fully'* – surely meant it was from Arno?

The proof presented itself in the handwriting. It was messy and pressed hard into the page. There was no disguising it. He'd once written her a poem on pink paper and the lettering was just the same. Arno. He was there in the handwriting. Could she let herself trust him again?

She pushed the note beneath her pillow to hide it. When she lay down again, she turned her head to one side so that her ear lay pressed into the cushion. As for *'Art and life meet in your aspect'* – what did it mean?

Her breakfast came a short time later – a single fried egg on a white plate with some vollkornbrot, which she refused to eat. The soldier boy was stood outside the open door. The blood on his shirt had been cleaned but a faint stain was still visible. It would stay there until he could afford to buy a replacement uniform.

'What day is it today?' Monika asked, trying to engineer a conversation with him.

The boy looked at her with a sneer. He seemed to have grown more bitter since his injury. 'Every day is the same here,' he said solemnly. 'You should eat your breakfast instead of asking questions. Hessen is coming to see you soon.'

'Why?'

'You're being moved. Something has changed. Don't ask me what.' The soldier boy brushed his hand through his blond hair as he walked away. 'Today is Thursday.'

Shortly after, Hessen arrived without knocking, but merely flung open the door and stood in the frame grinning avidly.

'Hello my ruby. I have some news. Your family have agreed to pay for your liberation.'

Monika looked up.

Hessen's smile slipped away quickly. 'The difficulty I face is that they have begun to connive. True to the form of your people, they have not offered what I asked for, but something else altogether. Just when I thought it was all going so smoothly, they do this. It is cowardly and dishonest, would you not agree, to try to fool me? But then, I don't suppose you know what I'm talking about.'

Monika turned her head with disdain.

Hessen rushed over and grabbed her by the back of her hair. He dragged her across the floor, as she grasped hold of his hand.

'Your release payment,' he shouted into her earhole. 'They are pretending that a painting they own covers the value of my request.' He then released her and took on a cordial tone. 'It's hard to believe,' – Hessen began to adjust his red armband – 'that they would consider this a reasonable substitute. It's rather like turning up to a roulette table with a handful of beans and saying they are magic. It's just not the way things are done.'

Monika listened closely. She was tired and listless, but her intellect was not blunted. She tried to make sense of this turn of events. The more she could understand, the better chance she had. A painting? As far as she knew, her family owned precious little beyond a couple of worthless oil landscapes and a few black-and-white engravings, the sort that anyone could buy from a market stall.

Then she considered another possibility, that her parents had acquired such an object from a family friend. But that would imply a debt to someone else? If so, it would be an act of desperation, the sort her parents would ordinarily avoid. Either way, they must have struggled to raise the ransom themselves.

Then she remembered the letter from Arno. The last line especially, which hardly sounded like him at all: '*Only to say, art and life meet in your aspect.*'

Art and life?

What was he trying to tell her? She braced herself as she made a risky decision. It was the only way to find out more. She spoke before she could change her mind.

'One of your men sent me this note.' She turned and reached beneath her pillow. Her heart began to pound uncontrollably. 'I thought you'd better know. I think he admires me.'

Hessen took the note and unfolded it. He read it quickly.

'Who gave you this?'
'One of the men here.'
'Which one?'

'I don't know. Not one of the soldiers. He was at the party. I've never seen him before.' She wanted to know who Arno was in Hessen's eyes.

'Ah!' Hessen smiled. 'The art collector. I see. He has a soft spot for you. Forgivable, if a little uncouth. But then what should we expect from someone who prefers painted images to real life?'

'An art collector?' she thought to herself.

'He's an ambitious young man trying to make as much money from your dirty people as he can. I admire that. But don't trouble yourself with the details.' Hessen held up the note. 'I shall correct him on his mistake.'

Monika watched as Hessen tore up the paper.

'Now, tell me: it's your people's New Year celebration soon, isn't it? I won't be celebrating with you, of course, but I have organised for five hundred of my best men to slap some faces as they come out of their synagogues. Which is exactly why you should feel better for being here.'

Monika wasn't listening to Hessen's threats. She was thinking about Arno. She knew there had to be a connection between him and the idea that her parents were attempting to use a painting as her ransom. She took a chance to give credibility to the idea.

'My parents do own a very valuable painting.'

'Is that so?' Hessen replied gingerly.

'It's been in the family for generations.'

A few moments later, a Stormtrooper appeared at the door. 'The clairvoyant is here to collect you. His car is outside.'

Hessen suddenly adopted a self-conscious expression, a sort of dignified pondering. 'Actually, let him come inside for a few minutes.' He turned to Monika to explain. 'Irregular as it sounds to some, I take advice from a psychic medium. He is quite brilliant.'

'Does he tell you what you should do with me?' Monika asked impertinently.

Hessen considered. 'You catch on quick. That is precisely what I intend to ask him. He is Danish by blood so he has Nordic insight. Not that you'd think so to look at him.'

Monika was taken from her room and led into a large office where Hessen's visitor stood with his back to a window.

'This is my spiritualist friend,' Hessen announced. 'Let me introduce you to Gustave Jan Ringel,' Hessen smiled. He was visibly pleased in the company of his associate.

The spiritualist stood with his hands linked behind his back, not replying to Hessen but maintaining his atmospheric silence.

Hessen approached the psychic and held him by the arms for a moment. 'Ringel has the ability to predict the future, which is extremely valuable, especially if you're prone to the odd wager as I am.'

'I have repeatedly foretold of events yet to occur, it is true.'

'My question to you is this: what should I do with this Jewess?'

'So, this is the girl you told me about?'

'Indeed she is.'

The clairvoyant approached Monika. His expression remained sombre, almost poised on mournful. He began to move his hands through the air, circling his fingers slowly around Monika's head. She flinched a little at his display. To her, the moment felt both alarming and utterly absurd at the same time.

'My feeling,' Ringel replied after half a minute, 'is that she is worth more than the ransom amount but you should release her. That, my dear friend, will bring about the best outcome for you. Now if I may, I would like to say one thing in private to this young woman.'

'You may,' Hessen said, oddly compliant towards the spiritualist.

Ringel now walked behind Monika and gently cupped his hand to her ear. 'Your fate is in my hands now.'

37

Early the next morning, Arno went out to telephone Monika's parents about their decision over the painting. Herr Goldstein confirmed that they had offered the alternative ransom to the kidnappers, who had since agreed and come back with further instructions.

Arno told Monika's father that it was the best decision and ended the call quickly. He then slipped out of the public phone box and took a meandering route back to his own place, trying to lose the pursuer that might or might not be following.

Despite it being only nine in the morning, he opened a bottle of beer. Then around mid-morning he heard a tapping sound on his attic hatch. He looked up and was startled for a moment to think that someone may have been waiting for his return.

He paused before answering and took a swig of beer. The tapping came again. Something in its less-than-insistent rhythm told him it was not the threat that he might expect. He drew back the hatch and was confronted with the face of Erich Ostwald looking up at him.

Arno asked the visitor up. Once inside, Erich made the *heil* salute, which Arno returned hastily. Erich was wearing his party uniform, a brown shirt, black tie and boots. He took off his cylindrical cap and loosened his tie. The two men stood in the middle of the attic floor. Erich looked pained, glancing around him as if he was thinking twice about his decision to come.

'Herr Ostwald,' Arno started up. He'd always used Erich's first name in the past, but with the Nazi standing inside his attic in full uniform, that no longer seemed appropriate. 'I'm pleased to see the Party is developing into a mighty machine. When the next elections come, we are sure to…'

'Forget about all that,' Erich interrupted. He was impatient, agitated. He rubbed his face. 'I can't stay for long.'

A ray of sunlight came blazing through the window. Erich paced left and right as if to avoid being caught by the beams.

'What do you want?' Arno asked.

'I came to tell you, I know about Monika. I know what she means to you.'

'I don't know anyone by that name,' Arno said bluntly.

'Don't bother lying to me. We don't have time for that.' Erich went on. 'I know you're not who you're pretending to be.'

Arno began to sense danger. Erich had seen through him – or was this some sort of bluff? A test? He took a step back. Erich had the edgy look of someone who intended to get to the truth.

'The exchange for Monika is happening tomorrow night,' Erich stated.

'Really? That sounds like a sordid business.'

'Admit it, damn it, the Jewish girl is important to you, isn't she?' Erich pounded the attic wall with the flat of his hand.

Arno's eyes flickered. He thought of the note he'd written to Monika. Had it been a risk too far? Had Erich seen it and now come to warn him off? Yet it hardly seemed enough to warrant a personal visit.

'The night of the Bavarian dancers. I confess, she caught my eye. What's the problem?' Arno said lifting his shoulders and palms up casually. He'd never seen Erich so agitated.

'I know that you're in a relationship with the girl. I also know you intend to offer a painting in place of the ransom.'

Arno was astonished by Erich's words. He felt suddenly defeated as if all he had been working to achieve threatened to collapse around him. There was nothing to be said in response. He picked up his half-drunk bottle of beer, ready to drink from it, ready also to use it as a weapon if the moment required.

'You've got it all wrong,' he began to say. 'Whatever you've been told about me…' He felt his fingers around the beer bottle tighten. The last thing he wanted to do was brandish it at Erich – but he would be prepared to if it came to it. He pictured himself doing it – smashing the bottle over the table edge and thrusting the splintered end under Erich's chin. He could do it in an instant.

Erich took a step back as his eyes moved to the bottle in Arno's hand.

'Listen, I've come to tell you that Hessen is in two minds about the painting. He really wants the cash.'

Arno moved towards Erich. There was no backing down now. 'Don't try and stop me.'

'Hessen has a lot of faith in his closest associates. Especially Ringel. He's the one who's persuaded him to accept the painting.'

'Why is Hessen so trusting of this fellow?'

'Because he is a master of disguise. A renowned psychic. He's a performer. I've seen him many times, he does mind-reading tricks and tells people's fortunes. He's very popular with the Party because they all think the future belongs to them. Ringel tells them what they want to hear.'

'What's all this got to do with Monika?'

'Hessen has massive debts and most of them are with Ringel.'

Arno remembered the letter he'd found on Hessen's desk begging for money.

'Ringel makes a small fortune from his shows and private séances. Hessen, on the other hand, has debts up to his eyeballs. Gambling, expensive indulgences like tailored clothing and his own personal racehorse. He comes from noble lineage, you see, and he likes to live the part. The trouble is, his appetite is bigger than his bank balance.'

'Is that why Hessen took Monika in the first place, because he's broke?'

'It's an easy earner for him. Besides he's an anti-Semite of the worst kind – hateful *and* opportunistic.'

'I don't believe taking Monika was opportunistic. It doesn't add up.'

'You're right. The day the police approached you…'

Arno slammed the bottle on the table and strode forward, grasping Erich by the throat. 'You know about the police? What else do you know?'

Erich wrestled with Arno as his grip began to smart. He managed to trip Arno up by winding his foot between his legs and behind his ankle. Arno rolled over, ready to start up again. He was livid.

'Wait,' Erich said, holding his hand up. But Arno didn't wait and punched Erich in the stomach. Erich then retaliated by ramming Arno into a wall. Erich scuffled over to the other side of the room and pulled the kitchen table out as a barricade between them. 'You were always too quick to use your fists!'

'What's the matter? Can't you keep up?'

'Oh, I can keep up. We can dance around all night. But we're wasting time.'

Arno went to the sink in the corner and tried to compose himself. He ran the tap and splashed water over his face. 'Speak then.'

'Arno, I know you've been working for the Prussian Police. Don't try to deny it. There's no point attempting to keep it a secret from me. What's more, the day you met the police, was also the day they persuaded Monika to go with them. They intentionally separated you both in order to recruit you. The way they saw it, if they could find a motivation to galvanise you, you'd be more willing to work for them. Except that they had an additional purpose for Monika – at least one of them did. The woman, Hannah Baumer, she handed Monika over to Hessen.'

'That's not right. Hannah Baumer works for the Prussian Police.'

'There are plenty who work for both – when the circumstances suit them. Hannah Baumer is just one of many. She was the one who took Monika.'

Arno began to feel the atmosphere shifting. Erich was revealing more than he expected, and seemed to have lost all allegiance to his Nazi comrades. 'What are you up to Erich?' Arno asked.

Erich gritted his teeth in resignation as his eyes turned to Arno. What was going through his mind?

'Who do you think I am?' Erich asked.

'I don't know – you tell me.'

'A Party member? A Nazi? Is that what you see?'

'Well, you're wearing the uniform.'

'The uniform? I may wear a uniform but it doesn't fit me. I'm still your old comrade. And the journey you have been on, I have taken it before you. I'm no longer with the Party, not underneath anyway. I haven't been for two years. I'm an informant now. I've been working to report on Hannah Baumer and anyone else who is exploiting their position in the police.'

'Are you telling me you're working for the same people as me?'

'I'm watching the likes of Hannah Baumer, so the answer is yes and no.'

'So Baumer is in league with the Nazis,' Arno thought to himself. And the man named Poelzig, he was connected to the Nazis too. Arno started to think it was him who planted the photograph and lured him out of the hotel. Poelzig was probably working for Baumer, meaning taking Monika was planned from the start.

'What about Vendetta? I thought you were in charge of Vendetta.'

'No one is in charge of it. Vendetta is a ghost. A mirage.'

'What does that mean?'

Erich paced in a circle as he unravelled his explanation. 'Vendetta is an invention by the upper ranks of the Party. What I have been doing is putting my weight behind it. That's been my means of establishing a role in the Party.'

'But what about the uprising?'

'There's plenty of dissatisfaction in the SA. The Stormtroopers are hungry for power and they run on that energy. Life isn't easy for these men. Half of them are out of work. The other half are rampant. They have a revolutionary mood about them and they're growing restless with all the political games. It's too slow-moving for them. They're afraid the Communists will beat them to the Reichstag. The whole point of Vendetta is to appease their restlessness, to make it appear as if the Nazi Party are planning a takeover of government. The thing is, Hitler decided long ago that the ballot box is the only way to real power, but a lot of men don't agree with him and think his strategy will prove fruitless. He's concerned about an internal overthrow. The idea stirs and seethes underneath everything. Vendetta is a way of keeping it in check.'

'So Vendetta is a foil?'

'All the work that goes into it is to feed the idea that it exists.'

Arno thought back to the paperwork he'd seen in Hessen's office – the transportation of weapons, soldiers and fake passports. 'So they've invented a whole network of agitators?'

'Precisely. It works for the Party to have the threat out there, alive, as it were against the Reichstag. As for me, I haven't disclosed any of this to a soul – not until now. Only a select few know the truth about Vendetta. The moment they consider an internal leak, I'll be a prime suspect.'

'Why are you telling me all this.'

'My position in the Party will be coming to an end soon. It's the right time for me to pass on what I know. Besides, I haven't forgotten how we worked together those few years ago. And if I can help you recover Monika, then I will.'

'There is one thing I need help with,' Arno said, as the significance of Erich's statements filtered through him. 'Göring. He mustn't be present at the exchange. I need him to take a one-way ticket out of Berlin. At least for the night.'

'What makes you think he will be present?'

'Because he is the art-lover of the Party, is he not? He had his eye on this painting before. It stands to reason he might be co-opted into proceedings.'

Erich scratched his ear, thinking. 'Well, Göring's wife

is ill. He's absolutely besotted with her – if you believe the syrupy crap peddled by Goebbels. Anyway, I heard she's gone to Stockholm to recover. A well-timed telephone call with news that her health has taken a turn for the worse can ensure that Göring is out of the way, if only for a few hours.'

'That's all I need. So long as he's not there.'

'Leave it to me,' Erich said, as he picked up his cap and fixed it on his head. 'I must go now but make sure you're ready for tomorrow night. Hessen will need all the persuasion we can give him.'

38

Tonight was *the* night. At seven o'clock Arno left his attic and travelled the city on foot. He made his way to Kreuzberg, where the bars were seedy and the prostitutes were bound to the streets like shackled slaves. When he approached the elevated S-Bahn station, he saw a lone figure stood beneath a street lamp smoking a cigarette, under the shadowy eaves of the iron structure.

Arno delayed his approach. Then the stranger tossed his cigarette onto the cobbled ground and moved away into the city. For a moment the station was deserted. The archways and iron girders that held the track above the ground led off both east and west as far as the eye could see.

Arno kept to the shadows of a doorway beneath a nearby apartment block. There he watched and waited for a sign as to what would happen next. A train came along the track and slowed as it entered the station, as if some great worm was burrowing into the earth. A few moments later, a trickle of passengers came down the stairway and spread out into the night, like marbles dropped onto a floor, rolling away in every direction. Across the street, a small baroque-style clock tower told the time: it was twenty minutes to eight.

Arno had risen early that day, not long after dawn, and made his way to Lassner's gallery. The Caravaggio painting, stored there for safekeeping, had to be transferred to the Goldsteins in preparation for the exchange. Lassner had received word and prepared the painting for transportation.

Having notified Monika's parents where the collection point would be, Arno took the painting to the Tiergarten. As planned, he cautiously left the object beneath a thicket of witch hazel, just off the main thoroughfare of the park, under the watchful eye of a withered, half-dead birch tree. A nearby fountain with a statue of Apollo facing east marked the spot. Herr Goldstein would obtain the package at exactly nine o'clock that morning.

Arno then laid low for the rest of the day. He returned to his apartment and spent his time making a written account of all he had discovered about the Vendetta plot. He left strict instructions for Thomas and hid the bundle on top of the loft joint as intended.

Over a plate of ham and sweet breads, he took a moment to track down his thoughts. He saw the hotel room from just two weeks before, when he and Monika were free, ignorant of the threat that was looming. He had little means of judging the course of things since then, except to admit that without the thought of reuniting with her, his resolve would have crumbled away a long time ago.

Stood now with his shoulder pressed to the grimy upright of a doorway with the S-Bahn station ahead of him, he scanned left and right. Suddenly a hand reached up behind him and he felt a squeeze on his left shoulder. He turned to find Erich pressed into the same doorway next to him. In a hushed voice, Erich said, 'It's time.'

The two men scurried across the open concourse of the road junction then passed over a lattice of tram lines and beneath the canopy of the station. On the other side of the construction, a small metal door was ajar. Erich tipped his head towards it, before Arno went first along a short passageway which led into a dingy room with a low ceiling. Two bulbs dimly lit a square space that was furnished with nothing more than a metal table and a rickety bench. Hessen was standing on the far side of the table and beside him were two SA soldiers. Arno noticed how all of the men, including Hessen, were armed with pistols.

He scoured the room for Monika. At first, he couldn't see her anywhere, not until his eyes became accustomed to the moon-white glare of the ceiling lights, at which point her form appeared as an ominous silhouette in the opposite corner. She was dressed all in black and had a shawl covering most of her head. Her hands were bound together at the wrists. She didn't look at him or say a word.

Hessen now addressed the room with its six inhabitants present. His message was short and perfunctory. 'Here it comes at last. Let us remain diligent in our purpose. Mistakes will be punished.'

Erich summoned one of the Brownshirts to follow him and gestured for Arno to come too. They emerged onto the street, at which Arno located the diminutive clock tower and read the time to be exactly eight. A passing train wobbled into the distance until there was quiet all around, except for the faint crooning of an accordion being played somewhere in the far distance.

Within the next minute, a pair of car headlamps came into view, approaching the junction at a steady pace. Travelling along the bullet-straight avenue of Skalitzer Strasse, the car seemed to take an interminable amount of time to reach them. Then as it came closer, one of the doors opened, from which a suitcase with rounded corners came into view.

The car began to slow as the suitcase was now extended almost entirely out of the door, and with an extra nudge, toppled from the ledge of the car. It tumbled over once, then skidded to a halt. The car drove on. Whoever was inside remained invisible.

The Brownshirt stepped forward and grabbed the suitcase. The three men immediately marched back through the doorway. In the room, the suitcase was lifted onto the metal table and its fasteners clicked open. The Brownshirt was told to stand outside as a lookout whilst the men examined the ransom package.

Inside the suitcase the painting was swaddled in its wrapping. Arno took it upon himself to step forward and examine the delivery. He opened the layers of felt wadding and eventually came to the canvas inside. It lay face-down as he drew back the last of the covering. When he turned it over, he was astonished to see that the painting before him was not the Caravaggio he had expected but a different picture altogether. He paused as a jolt of shock ran through him.

He looked up at Erich, then at Hessen. Without the Caravaggio, he hesitated over what to do next. The men around him waited for his response. He looked down at the painting again and tried to place it. How had the paintings got mixed up? It was the last thing Arno expected – or wanted.

'Well?' said Hessen.

Arno said nothing. He would have to improvise. Then he realised he'd seen the image before. It was the prized possession of Mattias Lassner, the very same work of art that Lassner had promised to set aside for his own retirement.

Arno lent over the painting and examined it by holding it up to the light. Next, he carefully turned it towards the room to show it to its prospective owner.

He now had a genuine work of art instead of the fake.

Hessen was on tenterhooks. 'Tell me. Your opinion? Is it good?'

'It is very good. Without a doubt,' Arno said, knowing it was now or never to act the show-off. 'This work is by Friedrich, one of our country's very best artists. Melancholy, yes, but deeply spiritual. He was alive to God's presence in every rock, tree and sunrise. I feel privileged to be in the company of such an object.'

'But what of its value?'

'At auction it would yield a very comfortable sum.'

'How much?'

'At least seventy thousand marks, and more on a good day.'

'I hope for your sake that's true,' Hessen said, as the Brownshirt stood next to him instinctively gripped his pistol.

'I'd stake my life on it,' Arno retorted. Then he noticed something poking out from between the folds of the painting's packaging. He tentatively reached for it, attempting to remain cool. Inside was an envelope with a short letter in Lassner's hand, along with an accompanying certificate of authenticity countersigned by no less than Hermann Göring. Arno looked over the letter quickly and then read it out loud.

'The artwork contained here within has been verified by the Mattias Lassner Gallery of Mulackstrasse, Berlin, as a genuine work by the eminent German painter Caspar David Friedrich. The work first belonged to Dr Otto Leopold Schudt from Dresden, acquired from the artist in the year 1822 in exchange for medical attention. Later passed on to his daughter, Theophila Schudt, and then by descent through the Schudt family. Later still to Hamburg and Berlin, it was acquired by the Goldstein family, where it has remained until the present day. Its current market value is

estimated to be between eighty and one-hundred-and-twenty thousand marks.'

Hessen took the letter and began reading it eagerly. When he looked up, he placed his attention entirely on Arno. 'One-hundred-and-twenty thousand marks.' There was a spark of excitement in his voice. 'That's what the letter says. I haven't heard of the artist, this Casper David Friedrich, but if Göring gives his assent…'

'The provenance too is excellent,' Arno added. He allowed himself the briefest of smiles as the weight of his task began to lift.

'You, girl,' Hessen said. 'Come over here.' He signalled Monika towards him. She came forward and stepped into the harsh glare of the electric lamps.

'This painting. Do you recognise it?'

Monika drew her shawl back a little. Arno saw her face in profile. His pulse quickened to see her put on the spot. 'Yes, I recognise it. It is the most valuable object that my family owns. It has hung in my father's study for many years.'

'Do you know anything about it?' Hessen asked.

'Not really,' she stammered.

'Come now. This is the most valuable object in your family and you don't know a thing about it?' Hessen inquired with lightness.

'I can furnish you with further details,' Arno said intervening.

At this moment, Hessen began casting his eyes around the room.

'Wait. Something has been bothering me,' Hessen said, turning to Arno. 'Maybe you could clear something up for me? You sent a note to the girl. I don't blame you for that, she has a certain basic beauty if you look closely. But ever since then I've been wondering why you acted like that. Why attempt to contact her with a secret note when you could have come directly to me? We're all on the same side, after all.'

'It was just a passing fancy. Nothing important to trouble you with.'

'No, that's not true. It's only now I see why you did as you did. You're concealing something from me. You think there is further opportunity to acquire from this family. That's why you're here this evening, not to assist me but to make sure the girl is released so that you can pursue her family for your own gain.'

'I can assure you,' Arno responded decisively, 'that I am only here to attest to the legitimacy of this painting. Nothing less, nothing more.'

Hessen passed a glance around the room. 'No, I don't think so. You suspect there is more to be plundered from this girl's family. This painting is just the tip of the iceberg. I wish you would have told me that sooner.'

At this, Hessen signalled to one of the Brownshirts with a quick flick of his head. The Brownshirt marched towards Monika and seized her by bracing her arm behind her back. Monika's face twisted with pain.

'She's not leaving,' Hessen declared. 'Not this evening anyway. I want a second painting. And then a third. And I want you to organise it. Bring them to me.'

'There is no second painting,' Arno said.

'You're lying to me.' Hessen's hand moved onto his pistol. 'Or is it that you really do admire this Jewess?'

Arno paused before saying anything further. The atmosphere in the room was spiralling out of control. He just had to get Hessen to change his mind.

'You must believe me. I don't have anything else to gain. You have my loyalty.'

Arno looked towards Erich, looking for any sign that

he was going to help. Erich said nothing.

'Stop talking,' Hessen said, pulling Monika forward. 'Or I'll give an order to break this girl's arm.'

'Wait,' Arno called out. 'I have something else that might be of interest.'

Hessen's eyes lit up.

'Your psychic. Ringel.'

'Ringel?'

'He claims to be a Danish aristocrat. But it's not true, is it?'

Hessen's grip on Monika slacked off as he attended to Arno's new line.

'Ringel is beyond reproach,' Hessen said.

'I wonder. Something told me he didn't quite fit. At the meal the other night, he was the only one not eating or drinking. It was odd. I didn't think anything of it, not until the following day when I learnt that it was a significant day in the Jewish calendar. A day when every Jew is expected to fast.'

'This is pure invention,' Hessen said with a scoff.

'I did some research. I found Ringel was on an old synagogue membership list – the synagogue has been demolished since then – under his former name. Gideon Krakovsky. He's a Silesian Jew. His father was the caretaker of the synagogue before becoming a travelling actor. His mother was a costume maker for the theatre troop.' Arno continued, observing he had Hessen's full attention. 'Ever since he started performing at La Scala, everyone in Berlin has believed his story. Except you. You knew he wasn't a Danish aristocrat but you kept it hidden, not for Ringel's sake but for your own. You daren't let anyone else in the Party know his real roots.'

Hessen's eyes remained fixed on Arno.

Arno decided to let him have everything he had.

'In February earlier this year, Ringel purchased a

Breslau printing firm and began publishing an occult journal, *The Ringel Newsreel*. He even featured your horoscope in its pages, didn't he? And you own a share of the journal, don't you? That's how he transfers money to you, through the company. And in return you maintain your silence. I discovered that your personal debts to Ringel are considerable. His debts to you are just as significant.'

'Not every Jew is without merit,' Hessen replied philosophically. 'At least Ringel is one of those who has chosen to serve the German people.'

'The truth is, if your relationship with Ringel was to come to light, then you would lose all your standing. In debt to your eyeballs to a Jewish magician who is little more than a charlatan. You would lose all credibility. Your position in the SA would no longer carry any weight. The Vendetta project would crumble under the loss of morale. Each and every one of your subordinates would consider you a fraud. As for your career in the Party, I doubt it would last more than five minutes after a scandal like this.'

Hessen looked as though he was going to explode but restrained himself.

'What do you want?' he asked.

'Let the girl go.'

Erich then went over to Hessen. 'This could ruin you and Vendetta. We cannot allow this news of Ringel to get out,' he whispered.

At this moment, the second Brownshirt lurched back into the room from outside. 'The car has turned around. It's making its return approach.'

Hessen nodded.

The Brownshirt untied Monika and took her by the arm, hauling her towards the door. Arno watched on, anguished but fiercely relieved. He knew Ringel would be

Hessen's weakness. The police findings he'd urgently inquired about confirmed what Arno had already suspected.

He wanted to take the Friedrich painting back but saw it could be trouble for Lassner. Besides he was unlikely to walk away with the new ransom payment even if it was the wrong painting.

He left the building and dashed out into the street to see if Monika was there, just in time to see her climb into the rear of the car. He watched the taillights of the Goldstein car pull away and swiftly diminish into the dark distance.

39

Arno slept for the entire night and day that followed. When the warm rays of August sunlight seeped through his window and slid onto his closed eyelids, he didn't get up. Scenes and events flashed before his mind's eye. He thought about *Trommler Gold* cigarettes, about African dancing girls at the Hopak Bar, about overnight train journeys and Hannah Baumer. He thought about Mattias Lassner and all those works of art. Most of all, he thought about lying in the hotel room with Monika and listening to her breathe, how she slept with immense stillness, as if her dreaming mind had completely taken leave of her body and had journeyed down to the centre of the earth.

A desire to contact her rose almost hourly, but he resisted. He thought he should give her a chance to come to terms with what she had gone through, for now at least.

The next day he finally left his attic room and went by the Goldstein household. Not to the front door but merely along the street where they lived. He chatted with the shoe-shiner and with a man who sold postcards of German beauty spots. He really wanted to see Monika and know she was okay. He wanted to explain.

Then the Goldstein's front door opened and he saw Monika and her parents coming out onto the street. He shielded himself behind a large oak tree and listened out for the familiar tones of her voice. She sounded different when she spoke to her parents. He heard laughter and then her father talking about taking a trip to the Delphi Kino to watch a film. He heard Monika reply that she'd like that.

He wanted to go over but something inside him caused him to stop. It was something he'd buried away ever since Monika had gone missing. The thing was shame. Shame of his Nazi past and how it had played a role in her abduction. In this knowledge, he withdrew.

That evening he returned to his attic room and collected his post. He found an envelope stamped with the insignia of the Mattias Lassner Gallery. Inside was a cash payment for his work at the gallery, plus a small dividend from the painting he helped to sell. The money was much needed – it would go on beer, food and last month's rent, strictly in that order.

When he thought about Lassner and the gallery, he realised he still had questions that needed answering. Lassner had given up his finest painting knowing it was going to Hessen. But why?

When Arno arrived on Mulackstrasse, he found Lassner sitting at his office desk with a new painting hung up on the wall in place of the Friedrich.

'Arno, my boy,' Lassner welcomed heartily as he laid his reading glasses on the table.

'There's something that I need to know,' Arno said, getting straight to the point. 'Why did you swap the artworks?'

'Well, what else could I have done? I could hardly let you enter the lions' den with a forgery.'

'You knew?'

'Oh yes.'

'But that painting was the security for your

retirement?'

'I suppose that's true.'

Arno took a seat opposite Lassner. 'Tell me, in the accompanying letter you said that the Friedrich painting had been acquired by the Goldstein family. How did you know about them? I didn't tell you anything?'

'No you didn't. But I knew of your attachment to Monika.'

Arno was baffled. 'There's only one set of people who knew about me and Monika.'

'Let's just say, I was briefed by the same people. Besides, I had another reason to swap the Caravaggio, not discounting the fact that it was a fake. Something, far more precious.'

Arno looked quizzically at the old gent.

Discreetly, from his inside pocket, Lassner took out a Jewish skull-cap and opened it briefly to Arno, as one would present a butterfly caught in cupped hands.

Arno realised his mentor was no Nazi.

Lassner looked around carefully. 'I have been providing information for six months now. The police could see I had penetration into the Party. I tell them when members come and go from the gallery, what cars they arrive in and with whom. Göring is of most interest, of course. Sometimes he brings a woman. Sometimes it's other party members. They're tracking his movements very closely.'

Arno sat back in his chair and took out a cigarette to light. 'Isn't it dangerous for you?'

'In the scheme of things I am insignificant to them. So are you. That's why the likes of you and me are perfect for this kind of work. Nobody suspects us because nobody thinks we are special. But that, my boy, is precisely why we are.'

Arno smirked to himself, knowing he'd been well-played.

Lassner's face remained serious. 'If these monsters get into power, people like me are doomed. Personally, I'm probably safe, so long as I can find them artworks to drool over. But Monika is part of the future generation of my people. I cannot put a value on that.' Lassner rose from his seat and walked towards the door.

'But using the fake would have worked,' Arno responded. 'I had some leverage over them.'

'I have no doubt you did, but I didn't want to take that risk. Besides, I won't be too surprised if the Friedrich makes its way home again. Now, if you'll excuse me, I have a luncheon appointment to go to. Come and visit us again, Arno. And if I hear of an opening for a gallery assistant, I'll be sure to recommend you.'

'I won't forget what you have done.'

Lassner smiled as he turned and squeezed Arno's shoulder.

Arno left the gallery and journeyed over to the other side of the city. He had his final written account detailing what he had discovered about the Vendetta plot. He delivered it to the derelict-looking postbox as prescribed by the police agent. He chose to omit any mention of Erich, not wishing to put Erich in any more jeopardy than he already was. The choice, however, turned out to be inconsequential, the reasons for which he learned later that evening when the pug-faced police agent made an unexpected visit to his attic.

At first, Arno found him just as brutal to look at as before, still bearing the same lumpy face and sunken eyes. Except, being out in the civilian world he seemed less formal and uptight. And he still had that perfect row of teeth. In a certain light, he was almost dignified. Arno had never known anyone so chameleon-like.

The two men went to a local bar, an underground wine cellar converted into a late-night drinking pit. They sat in a corner booth more or less out of sight. The agent spoke first and to the point, his white teeth flashing like fish in a moonlit river.

'I came to tell you that Erich Ostwald has become known to us as a field agent. He's been working undercover for the military intelligence, the *Abwehr*. They aren't meant to exist of course, not since Versailles. Their operation is small but very active.'

Arno listened – none of this was a surprise, but what came next was.

'His information on Hannah Baumer, along with his work on Vendetta, has put him in a very precarious position. As far as we can tell, Baumer discovered Erich's real identity and informed her superiors in the Nazi Party. Von Hessen certainly and others too I believe. Erich's life is now in great danger.'

Arno was roused but he tried to remain nonchalant. 'Why are you telling me?'

'You've been discharged from your duties to us.'

'I've discharged myself,' Arno interrupted.

'Either way, it's possible that Erich Ostwald will make contact with you. He may be looking for backing from within the Party, and you will be one of his better options. Otherwise, he may try to disappear. If he does, he might come to you for help.'

'And what do you expect me to do if he does?'

'If Ostwald comes to you,' the agent replied, 'tell him that you've left the Party and that you're not working for anyone anymore. You'll be of no use to him then.'

'Fine. Now why don't you tell me about Monika Goldstein?' Arno said, changing the subject. 'If it wasn't for your attempt to recruit me, she wouldn't have gone through such an ordeal.'

'The blame for Monika Goldstein's fortunes must lie with Hannah Baumer. She betrayed Monika. She betrayed all of us.' As he said this, a tone of genuine regret entered the agent's voice.

'And what about Hessen? Will he face charges?'

'The Prussian Police are doing all they can to monitor Von Hessen. But with the *Abwehr* involved now, we have to wait.'

Arno sat back in his seat. He would like to know more about the messy intricacies of police informants across Berlin. Then again, he knew it was a far better thing just to stand up, walk away and never set eyes on this ugly dog again.

Before he did, he had one last question, something that had been bothering him for all this time.

'That old photograph of me, the one where I'm stood with the Nazi youths, you showed it to Monika didn't you?'

'Well, what do you think?' the agent said, blinking a few times before taking a loud slurp of his drink.

'How did Monika respond when she saw it?'

'She said nothing. If anything, she wanted to defend you. But it was persuasive enough for her to come with us willingly, in the end.' The agent got to his feet. 'I'll leave you now, Herr Hiller.'

It was after midnight by the time Arno made his way back to his attic room. The agent had disappeared into the city, not before sliding another packet of cash across the table, his way of buying Arno's silence.

Alone again, Arno felt the chaos that had gripped his life for the past week and a half begin to ease. Most of all, as he took to his attic room bed, he thought of Monika. What did she think of him now? Did they still have a future? Tomorrow he'd travel to her house and find out.

How long had she been away? The calendar said ten days, but to Monika it felt like a whole year had passed. The world seemed hardly changed. Perhaps the young black cat from next door had grown a little, but that was all. It was extraordinary that life around her could go on as normal while she felt so altered.

Her parents made a great performance over her being home, serving her favourite foods and having long conversations about holidays the family would take during the year to follow. 'The future will be better,' her father said at least a dozen times.

As a gift, her parents bought her a new photo camera, a Leica Luxur with three interchangeable lenses. She cherished the object for it seemed to offer a particular type of hope where nothing else could. The act of placing her eye to the viewfinder and seeing the world framed, crystalline and somehow honest at that moment, made her recognise how fleeting time was and how the future was something perpetually unknown.

The first day of Rosh Hashanah was approaching. The family would go down to the Fasanen Strasse Synagogue just off the Kurfürstendamm to celebrate. The magnificent synagogue always reminded her at first of a Roman temple with its rounded archways and big triangular pediments. That is, until they got inside and stood beneath the golden domes with their millions of mosaics reminiscent of a Byzantine basilica.

The truth was, she was pleased to be back home with her parents, but she was also finding their attention suffocating. They had hardly left her for a moment since she had returned; they were doing their best and in some ways seemed to blame themselves for what had happened, but she craved solitude.

Alone in her room, she stood before her window and looked at the entwining branches of the lime trees and the church spires poking holes in the shifting sky. She held her camera in her hands; an unwavering witness to her small quarter of Berlin.

In those moments, when all she had were her own thoughts, her mind was filled with Arno. It was no use sitting indoors all day waiting for his call. She grabbed her cloche hat, pulled it low over her forehead and slipped out of the house unseen. She moved briskly down the street, with the rumble of trams in the near distance and the tall buildings rising up either side of her. Feeling exhilarated, she took off her hat and undid the top button of her dress.

She found herself at the Bayerischer Platz U-Bahn station, pausing as she recognised the recklessness of her actions. But before she might turn around to go back home, she looked up and saw Arno standing outside the station.

He saw her too. He stood tall and vivid. Now, facing each other, they looked silently across the open space. Memories stirred like a breeze rippling the surface of a lake. In that moment, neither of them had the choice of turning away. Everything around them became invisible as they walked towards each other, not knowing what would happen next.

FIND OUT MORE

Thank you so much for reading Monika and Arno's story. I hope you enjoyed your time with them in Berlin in 1931. If you enjoyed this book, please consider leaving a review on your chosen vendor.

Would you like to read more? I have an epilogue to *Vanished in Berlin* available for you to download.

Find out what happened next in Monika and Arno's story:

Download the epilogue for free:
https://dl.bookfunnel.com/3ltwc5481t

The final instalment of the Berlin Tales series, *Berlin Vengeance*, is available to read on the Kindle or in paperback:

https://books2read.com/u/47YwOE/

Thank you, and hope to see you again soon.

Christopher P Jones

To find out more, go to www.chrisjoneswrites.co.uk

THE BERLIN TALES

Berlin Vertigo
Vanished in Berlin
Berlin Vengeance

Printed in Great Britain
by Amazon